The Horses of Follyfoot

Monica Dickens

The Horses of Follyfoot

Piccolo Pan Books
in association with Heinemann

First published 1975 by William Heinemann Ltd
This edition published 1977 by Pan Books Ltd,
Cavaye Place, London SW10 9PG
in association with William Heinemann Ltd
© Monica Dickens 1975
ISBN 0 330 25216 X
Printed and bound in Great Britain by
Cox & Wyman Ltd, London, Reading and Fakenham

one

The colt, Folly, son of old Specs, was two months old that year when spring first came to the farm on the hill where the old horses lived at peace.

It came late and suddenly, taking everyone by surprise. For weeks it had been raining, steely, penetrating rain that made the older, thinner horses like Lancelot and Ranger shiver and cough if Dora or Steve or Callie left them out too long.

Dora and Steve were employed at the farm to look after the twenty horses who had been rescued from cruelty or neglect, or brought here by fond owners to end their days in peace. Callie's mother Anna had married the Colonel, who owned Follyfoot Farm. Callie was unpaid, but she worked just as hard as the others whenever she was free from the hindrance of school, which interfered with the real purpose of her life: the horses.

Lancelot was twenty-nine – the oldest horse in the world. Callie was determined to keep him alive to see thirty. If it was true that you multiplied a horse's age by seven to compare it with a person, he would then be two hundred and ten years old.

Bringing him in from a short leg-stretcher one wet afternoon she put hay on his back under a rug and made him a bran mash, spiced with salt and laced with molasses for energy. He stood steaming gently into the rug, with his ugly coffin head in the manger, his rickety legs gone over at the knees and under at the hocks, mumbling at the warm mash with his long yellow teeth.

'Pegging out at last.' Slugger Jones, the old ex-boxer who had worked for the Colonel for years, looked over the door of

Lancelot's stable, where Callie was brushing the mud from the old horse's legs with a wisp of twisted hay.

'Shut up,' said Callie. 'He's got years yet.'

Slugger made a jeering noise from under the wet sack that covered his balding head from the rain. 'He's older than me, the beggar.'

'Impossible.'

Callie came out of the stable. Slugger kicked out, but his boot was too caked with mud to lift far enough to catch her. Everybody's boots were permanently mud-logged at the end of that wet winter. It was not worth hosing them off. The whole farm was a sea of mud. Every gateway was a squelching morass.

Callie's hair was seaweed. Dora's short hair clung in wisps round her blunt brown face. Steve's black hair stuck out in wet spikes. Ron Stryker, who worked at the farm when the fancy took him and the Colonel could stand him, had long red hair which hung damply in his eyes. When Callie's mother gave him a rubber band to tie it back so that he could see what he was doing, he said, 'What I'm doing is mostly shovelling manure, and I'd rather not see.'

Then suddenly, from one day to the next, the rain was gone. A light fresh wind swept a curtain of last big drops over the farm and away down the hill, with the sun chasing it. You could see the rain still grey in the valley, and behind it, the broad sunlight painting the fields and hedges and the tops of the greening elm trees. Mist rose from the ponds and the river.

One of Callie's jobs was to look after the colt Folly and his mother. Old Specs had had her baby very late in life, and had almost died doing it. Callie had been keeping them in during the bad weather. When she turned them out into the first sunshine, the little bay colt went frisking and bucketing away on his silly long legs. Specs went after him in a series of feeble

6

bucks and squeals, stopped in the middle of the field with her head up and her nostrils spread to catch the messages of the spring breeze, then collapsed to roll and wallow in her favourite substance – sticky mud.

Anna's daffodils were rioting away under the trees on the lawn. The Colonel put away the dreadful old jacket he wore in the winter, with the leather patches on the elbows and cuffs. Ron Stryker bought a fancy pair of boots, which were too good to work in, but too tight to take off. Solution obvious: don't work.

Dora washed her jeans. It was worth it now. Steve's hair lay down again. Slugger took the sack off his head and put on his woollen cap. The grey stable cat decided to have her kittens early, in the bottom of an empty bran sack. The Colonel's mongrel dog had six big yellow puppies on Steve's bed in his room over the tack room.

Cobbler's Dream, the half-blind show jumping pony, hopped through a weak spot in the hedge and went mad in Mr Beckett's clover. The vet and the blacksmith sent in their bills at the same time. Ron fell in love with the new girl at the Silver Stud Café on the London road. Dora and Steve and Callie decided to hold a horse show to celebrate this glorious late spring.

two

As soon as the school closed for the Easter holidays, Dora and Callie rode round the neighbouring villages to announce the show among the local horse and pony population.

The kind of people who came to Follyfoot shows didn't go to proper shows, because they didn't have the proper kind of ponies, or because they didn't like shows. They just liked to ride.

Dora didn't even have a proper horse. Hero was lame again – legacy of his bad days with an evil-tempered lady in the circus. Callie rode Cobby, and Steve was off in the other direction on the chestnut Miss America.

Dora rode Willy the mule in the hard military saddle that made you understand why they had to mechanize the Army. His trot was like a truck with one flat tyre. His canter loosened your teeth. To turn him away from home, you had to lean forward, grab the rein near his mouth and pull it out sideways. If that didn't work, you had to go home.

Dora dreamed of a horse of her own, finely bred and schooled, a joy to ride or watch. Meanwhile, because she lived at Follyfoot, she made do with Willy, or stiff-legged Hero, or Stroller sitting sideways, because his back was as broad as the beer barrels he used to pull in his old days at the brewery.

Callie and Dora stopped at the Three Horseshoes to tell Toby to bring his Welsh pony. They went to the forge to tell the blacksmith's daughter to come with Pogo, and through the wood to the pony farm, whose owner was infested with swarms of horsy girls, some his, some not. On the way home they passed a house where a spindly roan horse was tied up in the yard, having ribbons plaited into its mane by two fat girls. The creepy Crowleys. They were famous at Callie's school for being the stupidest family ever seen in those parts.

'Don't ask them to come.' Callie jerked her head to where the girls were waving hopefully.

'They couldn't. That horse is lame.' Dora knew everything about every horse for miles round.

'That wouldn't stop them.'

The small field behind the Dutch barn had dried out enough for the show. The races would be in the middle and the jumps round the outside. Jumps at Follyfoot were not post and rails with white painted wings, or neatly clipped brush, or red block walls, the kind that Cobbler's Dream had cleared so nobly in the days when he was County champion. Follyfoot jumps were made of anything available. Fallen trees, oil drums, broken wheelbarrows, bits of old fencing. One class was called 'Back Alley Jumping' and it did indeed involve dustbins and broken chairs, a couple of old bicycle wheels which you could set spinning on the wings of a jump to test a pony's nerve, one of Anna's aprons flapping from a bar, a torn blue horse rug laid on the ground to simulate water, bales of hay and an old door. Ron dragged home some car tyres, bouncing along the road at the back of his motor bike.

'Where did you get those?' Dora and Steve walked through the yard with the mattress off the spare bed for the Refusal race.

'Down the road.'

'At the garage?'

'If you say so.' Ron never looked directly at you when he spoke.

'Didn't they want them?'

'I dunno. Didn't ask them, did I?'

The morning of the show, Anna came out to see where her washtub had gone.

'Apple bobbing.'

'Oh well.' Anna saw the mattress. 'Oh no, you've gone too far.'

Callie tried to turn her round and push her back towards the house. 'It's for the Refusal race. Don't fuss.'

Callie's narrow face was pale and fussed between the pigtails. Organizing things exhausted her, and she would throw up from excitement before the show. Everyone knew that. They would not start the show until she had.

The Colonel came out to see where all the pencils had gone from his office.

'Letter race. You gallop to the end of the field, get off and sign your name, race back and post it in the bird feeder on that tree.'

'Sounds pretty dull.'

'Not when you do it bareback, on someone else's horse,' Dora said. 'You're doing it on Willy.'

The Colonel groaned.

'Oh please, you must. It gives people something to laugh at.'

'I don't think Earl Blankenheimer does laugh.'

'Who's he?'

'Friend of mine from America. He's coming to see the farm.'

'Who is?' Anna asked.

'Old Blank. You know. He was with me in the hospital last year.'

The Colonel's old war wound played him up sometimes. He would cough painfully for weeks, until Anna got desperate, and Slugger, who had once saved him from being burned alive in a tank, bullied him into getting some treatment.

'He was in the next bed to me, remember?' the Colonel said. 'Nice enough chap. He was over here looking at 'chasers. Went to the Newbury meeting. It rained for three days. He got pneumonia, more fool him, to come to England in February, and ended up in hospital. He's over here now, looking at a stallion he might buy.'

'Racehorse breeder?' Ron pricked up his ears. A racing stable was more his line than a home for old horses.

'In a small way. Got a bit of money, I believe, though I don't think he knows much.'

'He don't know nothing till 'e's seen the great Follyfoot horse show.' Ron swept an arm round the field with its collection of washtubs, laundry lines and bizarre back alley jumps.

three

About twenty people came to the horse show. There was Toby, the funny little undersized boy with the goblin face and pointed ears, whose father kept the Three Horseshoes. He had a swarm of brothers and sisters. Nobody had ever been able to get them together in one place for long enough to count.

When people asked Toby's mother why she had so many children, she replied that she'd had to have a lot, hadn't she, or she wouldn't have enough older ones to take care of all the babies.

Toby's mother didn't always make much sense. His father made sense with the back of his hand. Sometimes when Callie got on the school bus, there would be a plaster on Toby's cheek, or a muffler round his neck to hide a bruise.

Toby had not had much fun in life before he met Callie and the people at the Farm, particularly the four-legged ones. Steve, who had taught him to ride, was his hero. He was in love with Dora. Callie was his best friend. Anna made doughnuts for him.

He was the only person who was not afraid of the Colonel, when something went wrong at Follyfoot. When the Colonel limped through the yard demanding to know how Stroller had got into Arthur Flagg's potato patch, or who had left a pitchfork in Ranger's stable or a saddle out on a fence all night, everybody else became very busy doing something vital. Ron Stryker, whose fault it usually was, disappeared into the pump house, but Toby stood his ground in the middle of the yard, leaning on a broom that was as tall as he was and inquired sunnily, 'You rang, Colonel?'

The Colonel liked that. In return, he revolutionized Toby's life on the day that the nurseryman said he'd gone motorized and wouldn't be coming back for his two Welsh ponies.

The grey one had laminitis, but the cream-coloured one was fat and safe, and the Colonel gave it to Toby. He kept it in a shed behind the pub. Its name was Coffee, because it coughed. It was almost wider than it was long. Toby rode with his short skinny legs sticking straight out on either side, and Coffee performed great feats for him of a slow and unambitious nature.

Some of Toby's brothers and sisters came to the horse show, fighting, screaming, whining or bellowing, according to age. His mother had two in a double pushchair and one on her back in a canvas sling. She always had a small baby at any time of year. Two last year when she had the twins.

The girls from the pony farm came through the wood and down the field track like a small army. The blacksmith's daughter, who had lost the use of her legs in a car crash, ambled down the road on her Fell pony Pogo. He was trained to stand quietly in a pit, so that she could pull herself on to his back from her wheelchair and ride him up the slope to ground level. Moll was a splendid girl with freckles and a loud laugh. When she fell off jumping the car tyres, she sat on the ground shouting with laughter until someone picked her up and put her back on Pogo.

A boy and a girl from the house at the bottom of the hill came up with their father's two elderly steeplechasers, who were retired to grass down there. Mrs Oldcastle, in old-fashioned ballooning breeches, cantered sedately across the fields from 'Rose Holme' on her large-footed cob named Harold. Two children pottered in on muddy Shetlands.

Hero was still lame, so Dora rode the mule. Steve rode Miss America, who had been rescued from a riding stable with a brutally sore back. She still could not take a saddle.

Callie, of course, rode Cobbler's Dream. He was pretty much hers now that Steve was too heavy for him. Ron refused to ride, because the girls from the pony farm laughed at him. He sat on a bale of hay at the side of the ring and did the Musical Sacks on his transistor, or squatted by jumps going, 'Kcheech!' to test the ponies' nerves.

Joe Fuller, who owned the pony farm, was the judge. To be fair, he tried not to let his ponies win too often. The show was constantly punctuated by clamouring groups of girls on New Forests and Exmoors going, 'Joe, it's not fair! But Joe, I won, you saw me! Oh please, let's run it again – come on, Joe!'

In the dog race, where your dog was supposed to follow your horse, two or three fights broke out to add to the clamour. Dora separated two dogs by flinging a bucket of water at them, bucket and all. Above the noise, she heard Callie shout at her, and saw her standing in her stirrups looking towards the road. Dora stood on a wheelbarrow and saw them coming.

One large girl riding the thin roan horse that might once have been a hunter, the other on a bicycle, fat legs in shorts revolving, the parents following in a car.

'The Crowleys.' She turned to Steve.

'They never.'

'They have.'

The Crowleys came in at the far gate, parked their car and began wiping down the horse with tea towels in an ostentatious and unnecessary way. From the back of the car, the mother unpacked an enormous amount of food and drink, which they did not offer to share with anybody.

When Dora rode down to that end of the field to practise Willy over the right-angled in-and-out jump, she saw the

Crowleys trying to make the roan mare jump the brush. Marcia, the sullenest of the girls, would ride up to the jump with a great deal of arm-flapping and leg-pumping. The mare, who was dropping her left hind leg in a painful way, very sensibly stopped dead before the jump. The child beat at her with a long stick, burst into angry tears, and changed the stick to the other side.

'That horse is lame,' Dora called out. 'You can't ride her.'

'Mind your own business.' Marcia turned her anger to Dora.

'Dopey's all right.' The mother had been throwing clods of turf at the mare's bony back end. 'She's just a little stiff when she starts up.'

'She's lame in that near hind leg.'

'She's always moved a little funny.' The father came up now with a bottle of ginger beer, moon-faced, the sun glinting on his round glasses. 'That's why we got her so cheap.'

'And the girls adore Dopey. They take endless care of her. Don't you girls? Don't you girls!' The mother shouted at her sulky daughters, who scowled back at her. 'She's a darling. We wouldn't hurt her for the world.'

'You are hurting her,' Dora said, 'You can't ride her in our show.'

Dora could be pretty blunt where horses were concerned. She did not especially try to be rude. It just came naturally.

'We've come all this way,' the father said.

'Let's go home,' whined Marcia.

'You're to have your fun,' the father ordered. 'Dopey will be all right. You'll see.'

'Yeah,' said Dora. 'We'll see.' And kept an eye on them.

four

In the True Love race, pairs of riders held a strip of paper between them to represent the marriage licence. When the paper broke, they were divorced and eliminated. Callie and Toby paired off. Dora wanted to go with Steve, but there was too much competition for him from the pony farm girls.

'Will you be my partner?' Amanda Crowley rode up on the roan.

'I told you, you can't—'

'She's all right now. I need a partner.'

'I've got one.' Dora hastily grabbed at the flare of Mrs Oldcastle's breeches.

Harold cantered steadily round the outside of the ring, as if he were on rails. The mule kept veering towards the middle of the field, since the Colonel was there as ring steward, with horse nuts at the bottom of his poacher's pocket. Dora and Mrs Oldcastle were divorced after half a round. So was Amanda Crowley, since Dopey was very slow, and the girl perched on the steeplechaser couldn't hold him back.

Dora bided her time.

In the Refusal race, you had to trot up to a jump, stop the horse and sail over the jump by yourself. On to Anna's spare room mattress. Easy for Dora, since Willy naturally refused any jump. The mule trotted up to the jump with his rough, wavering gait and stopped dead with his neck out. Dora hurled herself through the air with her eyes shut, landed on her back on the mattress, and looked up into a startled face under a brand new green sporting cap, worn dead straight.

'Hullo,' said Dora. There was nothing else to say.

'Oh – hi there,' the face said uncertainly. 'I – er, I'm looking for the Colonel.'

'Over there.' Dora scrambled to her feet. She nodded to where the Colonel in shabby old clothes was lolling on Stroller's bare back, his unlit pipe in his mouth and his hat tipped over his eyes against the sun.

'Could have fooled me,' said the stranger. He must be the American from the hospital.

When Dora called, the Colonel slid off Stroller and came across with his large brown hand held out.

'Blankenheimer, my dear chap. It's good to see you.'

Mr Blankenheimer shook hands with him and stepped quickly out of the way as Willy, unpredictable as all mules, suddenly decided to jump after all. He came over in his fore and aft fashion, front end on its own, back end following a bit later, landed on the mattress, put his foot on his reins, threw up his head, broke the rein, wandered away and bit Coffee in the rump.

Mr Blankenheimer laughed nervously. 'Quite a circus you have here.'

'Great, isn't it?' The Colonel had not even stepped out of the way as the mule jumped, just bent his tall frame slightly sideways. 'It's our spring horse show.'

'Oh, pardon me.' The American was all dressed up as if he thought it was a real horseshow: a bright jacket, shirt and tie with a foxhead pin, crisp trousers, jodhpur boots that squeaked.

He was rather nice. He was gentle and eager to please. He smiled a lot, and cheered mildly and clapped. In the relay race, when everyone yelled for the ponies, not the riders – 'Come on, Pansy! Get going, Coffee!' – he yelled too: 'C'mawn Cawfee!'

He helped to put up jumps. He sat with Ron on a bale of hay, sucking a wisp of it and discussing the odds on the 3·30 race at Sandown. He held ponies for people who were soaking their faces in the apple bobbing. He poured cider for Anna in the nosebag race. You galloped to one end of the ring, grabbed a doughnut off a string with your teeth, and ate it before you got back to the other end, where you were handed a cup of cider, and had to trot back without spilling it. Then you drank it, if there was any left.

'More fun than a barrel of monkeys,' was the opinion of Mr Blankenheimer.

In the last jumping event, Amanda Crowley brought poor Dopey on to the course, carrying the long stick.

The Colonel put out a hand and caught the roan mare's rein as she turned her towards the first jump. 'No whip.' He took it away from her.

'She won't jump without it,' the girl protested. 'She's a pig.'

'No,' said the Colonel mildly. 'She's old and tired.'

He let Amanda have three tries, since he knew the horse would not jump. After the third refusal, he silently handed her back the stick, and she rode angrily back to get some food out of the back of her car.

'Look here.' Mr and Mrs Crowley were on the scene. 'It's not good enough.'

'To jump her, it isn't.' The Colonel was good at protecting horses from people like this. 'Dora's right. The horse is lame behind.'

'All very well for Dora,' the mother said, some spite looking out of her small black eyes above the swollen cheeks. 'She's got a stable full of horses to ride.' (Willy? Lame Hero? Spot, whose back was too broad and flat to do anything but stand on it? The shetlands?) 'My girls have only Dopey.'

'*And* spoil her to match.' The father had a manner part aggressive, part whining. 'Gone without, we have, to feed this animal. I'm not a rich man, Colonel, as you know, but I'll not have it said . . . Gone without meat on the table . . .'

'Horses don't eat meat.' The Colonel was easily bored. He had stopped listening.

five

At the end of the show, when Mr Blankenheimer was present-
ing the rosettes made by Anna out of Christmas paper, a small
commotion made itself known at the far end of the field.

One of the Crowley girls, long stick in hand, had somehow
beaten the roan mare into the in-and-out, and was trying to
beat her out again.

Steve rode Miss America fast to the end of the field, jumped
off, and into the in-and-out, grabbed the stick and whacked the
Crowley girl across her fat rump.

'He hit me – ai – ai – ai!'

The father let out with his right fist and punched Steve in
the face. Steve punched him back, and then they were down
together, rolling about on the ground between the jumps, the
roan mare nervously lifting her feet so as not to step on them.

Dora could only stand and watch from a distance. Steve had
been in trouble before for fighting. When his temper was
strong, he could really hurt somebody. Mr Crowley was lucky.
He wriggled away, got up, shouted to the Colonel that he
would sue him ('I'll be suing you,' added Ron), and left the
scene.

'Will they really sue?' Mr Blankenheimer had watched the
drama with his eyes popping under the green cap.

The Colonel grunted impatiently. 'It's just talk. Always
looking for trouble. That's the way they live.'

'Are all English horse shows like this?' the American asked.

'Yeah, sure,' said Ron. 'You ain't seen nothing yet. Stick
around, mate.'

Dora liked this small gentle man. 'Come on, I'll show you the rest of the horses.'

'Oh dear.' He looked at his watch in the fussy way of a man ruled by time. 'I can't. I have a business appointment.'

'To see the stallion?' Dora would like to go too.

'No, Miss – er.' He had been too shy to call anybody by name yet, except when he was shouting for the ponies. 'To see some – er, tiling. I'm here on business too. The construction business. I'm after some of your laminated, self-adhesive, mosaic. You folks are way ahead of us, I have to tell you.'

'Thanks.' Dora was out of her depth. 'Can you come back tomorrow and see the horses?'

'Could I?' Mr Blankenheimer beamed at the favour. It was really a favour for Dora. She never got tired of showing off the horses and telling their histories. 'This is Puss, who was being ridden to London with a petition for the Queen . . . this is Ginger, who used to pull a milk cart . . . this is poor old Frank – see the dent in his head from the tight halter . . .'

He was back the next day in his stiff, formal clothes, coming as uncertainly into the yard as if he were an unwelcome tax collector.

The Colonel was trimming feet. He greeted Mr Blankenheimer from an upside down face, without letting go of Dolly's back foot. Once you let it down, it was hard to pick up again. Mr Blankenheimer seemed a bit nervous of him. He stood and watched, and folded his arms, and put his hands in his pockets, and then behind his back, and cleared his throat, while the Colonel went on paring with his sharp curved knife, making the whistling hiss between his teeth with which all the horses were so familiar. The Colonel was shy too, and when he was with another shy person, it could be paralysing. Dora, rescuing Mr Blankenheimer to begin his tour of the inmates, wondered what the two of them had talked about, trapped in that green hospital room with the high beds and sterile smells.

All the horses were out except Lancelot, who had one of his groggy spells today. He would rather be groggy indoors, than outside where the others would bother him.

Some people thought Lancelot was ugly, with his bony frame and patchy skewbald hide, but to Dora he was beautiful.

'He'd be dead if it wasn't for Follyfoot,' she said.

'Some folks would say he should be put – er, put to sleep,' Mr Blankenheimer said sadly.

'The Colonel doesn't believe in taking a horse's life if he can still enjoy it,' Dora said. 'That's half the point of this place.'

'It's splendid,' Mr Blankenheimer said. 'Very fine. A Home of Rest for Horses. How British can you get? You could never have a place like this in the States. We're too practical about horses over there. Not sentimental.'

'Not crazy, you mean.' Steve came out of Hero's stable pushing a barrow with a rickety wheel. It had been on the brink of collapse for months. A lot of the equipment at Folly-foot was old and groggy, like Lancelot. But the Colonel was plagued with bills for winter feed and bedding. When the barrow wheel let go and tipped its load almost on Mr Blanken-heimer's neat feet, Steve sighed, and went off to the tool shed for some dowelling to mend the wheel again.

Dora took the American round the fields and showed him the horses and told him how each one had come here. He thrilled to the story of Callie stealing Hero from the circus, and when he heard about Ranger, whose jaw had been half torn off by a cruel wire bit, his eyes filled with ready tears.

She told him how Folly had been born in a ditch where Specs was trapped, and how Cobbler's Dream had found them.

He was fascinated. He loved the idea and the ideals of Folly-foot.

'Wouldn't it be wonderful if—'

'If what?'

'Just a dream, I guess, Miss – er—'

'Dora.'

She could not call him Earl. Nor Mr Blankenheimer. She called him Mr Blank.

Since he was a racehorse owner, she showed off Folly proudly.

'Look at that length from croup to hock.' She made the shrewd face that people make when they size up horseflesh. 'And see the muscle here already.' Dora gripped the negligible crest of Folly's young neck, and the colt struck out with his narrow hoof and ducked away. 'Look at the bone on him, look at the bone.'

'I'll say.' Mr Blank narrowed his eyes and imitated Dora's shrewd face. He did not know much, but he had a natural feeling for horses. He did not laugh at Dora, like the last visitor who had said, 'Doesn't it bother you to feed these old nags when half the world is starving?'

He wanted to go into the hay barn, to remind himself of his boyhood in Indiana.

'I love places like this.' They sat down on a bale of hay and inhaled the dusty sweet smell of outdoors preserved indoors which gave the barn its special atmosphere. The old beams were curtained with cobwebs, the floor stamped into troughs and hollows by generations of working feet.

'Where my racehorses are, it's all so grand. I don't even know where they keep the hay. It's too tidy. Where I keep my daughter's horse, they don't even feed hay. Just roughage pellets. On schedule. You can't bring carrots or sugar in your pocket.' He sighed. 'You know, Dora, I'm glad it was you showed me around today. You're kinda – kinda old shoe.'

'Thanks,' Dora said. 'Thanks, Mr Blank.'

'Why do you call me that?'

'It suits you.'

'You think so?' He turned an unhappy face to her. 'You think I'm a nothing?'

'Of course not.'

'Other people do. They don't pay me too much notice.'

'Look at it this way, Mr Blank.' Dora thought quickly. 'There was a blank in my life, and you fill it.'

'Gee. Wow.' If she'd handed him a thousand pounds, he could not have been more pleased. Especially since he didn't need a thousand pounds.

They seemed to have made friends. She'd call him Blank. He'd call her Door.

'I like you, Blank.' Dora had not made a new friend for ages.

'I like you, Door.'

Blank Door. A code name. 'No Handle.'

On the way to get his car, they took a detour to see the last few horses in the top field. Magic, the black police horse, was grazing peacefully with the sun on his round shining quarters and his full tail swishing rhythmically.

'He's twenty-five,' Dora said. 'Been on the streets almost all his life. Riots. Parades. Traffic. He's done his work. Now he's enjoying his rest.'

'My gosh,' Blank said. 'That old guy looks fitter than a lot of horses who are still working. Look at that roan horse there was all the trouble about yesterday. This is where that one ought to be.'

'I know,' said Dora. 'I wish we had her.'

'If she had her way,' Slugger had come to lean over the gate with them, 'half the horses in the county would be up Folly-foot Farm.'

'It's agony though,' Dora said. 'People are so stupid. I

suppose they mean well, but they have all the wrong sort of sentiment, creeps like the Crowleys. I wish we could get them to see that Dopey shouldn't be ridden. Dopey – what an insult to a horse. I'm sure the Colonel would take her here.'

'Oh my Gawd.' Slugger pulled his woollen cap down over his best eye.

Dora grumbled on about the Crowleys. 'They're always carrying on about not having meat on the table and how they starve themselves to feed the 'dah-ling' horse. But one look at those fat pigs, and you know who comes first in that family.'

'If they want meat, they could shoot the horse and put him on the table then, couldn't they?' Slugger's jokes could be pretty sick.

'Shut up.'

'Now, lookit—'

Door and Blank spoke together. They exchanged a No Handle look of understanding.

'What are you planning?' Slugger lifted the edge of his cap to see.

'Nothing,' said Dora. 'I wish I was.'

'Gawd help us all,' said Slugger.

six

After Blank had driven away in his hired car, turning to wave and grazing the gatepost, Dora still could not talk at supper about anything else but Dopey.

'I've still got that poor mare on my mind,' she said, sitting at the round kitchen table, picking at Anna's meat pie.

'And I've still got that man's knuckles on my face.' Steve rubbed his cheek, which had come up into a bruise of interesting colours.

'It is awful,' Dora fretted. 'That horse will never be sound, and those dopes will never give her up. I wish we could steal her.'

'You've stolen enough horses in your day,' Steve said. 'Britain's number one horse thief, you are. If you'd been sentenced for all the horses you've stolen or swindled people out of, you'd be doing hard labour for the next two hundred years.'

'That would be good.' Callie looked up. 'Then she could go down the mines and work with the ponies.'

'Women don't work in mines, stupid.' Steve kicked her under the table.

'I wish they did.' Callie made a toad face at him. 'Then I could go and work with the pit ponies.'

'They don't have ponies in mines any more, stupid.'

Callie sulked. Sometimes it was hard being the only child among grown ups. But when her mother asked her if she would like to have friends to stay, she couldn't think of anyone to ask. She didn't really have friends, except Toby. The horses were her friends. And Dora and Steve, and Ron when he wasn't being mean.

Sometimes they treated her like a silly kid. At other times they loaded a whole lot of work and responsibility on her. Her father would have understood. When your father is dead, it's easy to daydream that he would have understood everything.

She pushed back her chair into the fireplace and ran upstairs to look at the picture of him over her bed, sitting loosely on his famous steeplechaser Wonderboy, who was still at Follyfoot, idling the last of his days.

Anna followed her upstairs and sat on the bed.

'I love that picture,' she said.

'How could you marry the Colonel,' Callie said, still sulking, 'if you still loved my father?'

'You were glad when I married him,' Anna said, surprised.

'Mm-hm.'

'And you're glad now, aren't you?'

'Mm-hm.'

'Well then,' said Anna.

'Well then,' said Callie, and sighed.

When Callie came back to the kitchen, Steve reached back and picked up her chair out of the fireplace without taking his fork out of the mashed potato. Callie often pushed her chair into the fireplace and ran out of the room. No one bothered to look up. They had all been through that stage. Dora went back to it sometimes, when things went really wrong.

She was still agonizing over the roan mare. 'Did you hear what he said? "I'm not a rich man, you know, Colonel." ' She imitated Mr Crowley's whining voice. 'I hate it when people cry poor.'

'Well, they are poor,' Steve said.

'So are we.' There was never enough money at Follyfoot.

The Colonel waged a monthly battle with the bills that silted up his office desk like river mud.

'I wish we weren't,' Dora sighed. 'I wish we could buy that mare, and take care of her here. If we made a really good offer—'

'If, if, if,' the Colonel said. 'You've got two dreams, Dora. One is about all the horses you could steal if you had the nerve. The other is about all the things you could do if you had the money.'

'I know. I'd buy this gorgeous bay thoroughbred. Two white feet. Small neat head with those sort of smily dark blue eyes. Stepping out really free. Fit and supple. All that muscle moving like cream ... Remember David, Steve, how he moved, and how he held his head, that natural flexion ...' She went off into a dream of beautiful horses, with her elbow on the table and her cheek in her hand.

'If you're not going to eat your pudding,' Callie said, 'I'll have it.'

In the night, Dora had a revelation. She got revelations sometimes in the night, and heard voices. She felt she must be psychic. Sometimes she heard horses neighing and the thunder of hoofs on hard hill turf.

Tonight she was into a dream of the open sea. She was swimming on a splendid horse, her arms round its crested neck, which was somehow part of the cresting waves. Suddenly, in her sleep or in her waking, a voice said very clearly, 'Door.'

She was wide awake in an instant, and sat upright. It had sounded just as if Blank were in the room.

That was the revelation. Blank had money. She would ask him to go to the Crowleys and buy the roan mare.

It was early, only just growing light, but Dora got up and

went down to muck out. She had to do something with the energy of her excitement.

At a decent hour, she telephoned Blank at his hotel.

'Could you possibly come up here right away?'

'Well gee, honey – Door – I don't know that I can. I have this guy to see about the recycled caulking strips, and—'

'It's an emergency,' Dora said. 'A matter of life and death.'

Blank's life did not normally hold such drama. He was up at the farm before Dora and Steve had finished the morning work. Dora had not told Steve yet. She didn't quite know why. Something about the money? Though he called her a horse thief, he had always shared in her plots and schemes of rescue. But somehow today . . .

When Blank came across the yard, she said, 'No Handle,' and pushed him into an empty loose box to tell him the plan.

He became very excited, but nervous too, his hands shaking, his eyes glancing from Dora to the door as if he expected to see a posse of sheriffs after him already.

'What'll I say?' he kept asking, even while she was telling him. 'What'll I say?'

'You can say you've seen this horse of theirs,' Dora repeated, 'and that you like his looks, and nothing will satisfy you but to buy him.'

She described the little patch of field where Dopey lived out her boring days on a bare patch of ground, with no shade.

'You can say you were driving by. You can say you're a mad American millionaire. Say you're the Mafia. Say your wife fancies the mare and won't be denied. Say anything, but *get that horse*.' She fixed him with a stern eye.

'Yes, Door, yes.' His eyes met hers at last. 'I'll do it.'

He went out of the loose box, walking with his knees slightly bent, shoulders rounded, fists clenched. Dora did not have to worry whether to tell Steve. Blank told him at once.

'I'm off on a mission of mercy, my boy.' He held out his hand. 'Wish me luck.'

'What has she got you into?' Steve took his hand and grinned at Dora.

'I got myself into it. There's no turning back. Wish me luck.' He held out his hand to Slugger, walking past with buckets. Slugger set down the buckets, wiped his hand on his baggy trousers, shook Blank's hand, picked up the buckets and walked on. Dora hoped Blank wasn't going to tell everyone he met on the way.

'Why didn't you tell me?' Steve asked Dora.

'I don't know. Something about it being money. What we've done before, it's been us doing it. We haven't used anyone's money. I thought—'

'With money,' Steve said, 'it's better not to think about it. Just either spend it or don't.'

Dora was good at creating complicated questions. Steve was good at giving simple answers.

After dropping Blank round the corner from the Crowleys, Dora and Steve took the horse box and waited in a side road some distance away. An eternity passed, during which they imagined Blank kidnapped for ransom, arrested, beaten up by Mr Crowley, poisoned by Mrs, forced to marry the oldest daughter Juliette, who was even fatter and stupider than Amanda and Marcia. At last they heard the faint sound of hoofs on the road. The hoofbeats grew louder, and Blank appeared round the corner of a hedge, leading the mare slowly, a smile of pure triumphant happiness on his innocent face.

'How did you do it?' Dora jumped down from the cab of the horse box.

He stopped, looked down, and scraped the gravel of the road with his toe.

'I charmed her,' he admitted. 'I really think I charmed her.'

'With money?' Steve jumped down and took the mare's halter rope.

'No.' Blank looked up. 'With my charm.'

'And how much money?' insisted Steve.

'More than I should have.' He looked down again. 'But it wasn't that easy. When Mrs Crowley asked me where I was taking the horse, I had to make up this story about a man delivering another horse for me, and how he would meet me on the road, and we would take the mare to this place I have, with all this good grass and so on. She wanted to know where, so I said Wales. It was the only place I could think of. "Oh," she says, "Wales, my girlhood home. Whereabouts?" "Well, I'm just moving houses." "Where to?" "Well, they've changed the name of the village because it was ugly, so I,—" "No Welsh names are ugly," she says. Phew!' He mopped his beaded forehead and shook his head. 'You know how when you start with one lie, you get into more and more? I had my fingers crossed in both pockets.'

Dora put her arms round Dopey's thin neck, as she sagged in the road, resting the lame hind leg.

'Thanks, Blank,' she said.

'My pleasure.'

'Isn't it fun to be a horse thief?'

'Hey, wait a minute, Door,' Blank said. 'I paid for that horse.'

'How much then?' Steve asked. 'Tell us.'

Blank named an outrageous figure, about twenty times as much as the poor old roan was worth, even for dog meat and sofa stuffing.

Steve whistled. 'With that money, you could have bought us a really super horse to ride.'

He was joking, but Blank turned on him a solemn look. 'But that's not the idea of Follyfoot, is it? I thought—'

'Of course not.' Dora patted his hand. 'You've caught on very quickly, Blank.'

seven

Mr Blank was in love with the whole idea of Follyfoot. He wished he didn't have to go back to America tomorrow. Instead of going to visit the manufacturer of stretchable caulking recycled from paper cups and used tea bags, he stayed to let Dora teach him how to muck out and put down clean bedding in the stable he prepared for his mare.

'So they've got you in the business, Blankenheimer.' The Colonel came and smiled over the door. 'Let's keep her in a bit till we see what we can do for that leg. What do you call her?'

'Not Dopey, that's for sure.' Blank bent down to tease straw around the mare's front feet. 'If she was a gelding, I'd call him Man-o'-War, after the most famous racehorse in the world.'

'Why not Woman-o'-War?' asked Dora.

'I like it.'

Dopey was rechristened Woman.

It was too late for Blank to keep his appointment with the tea bag man, so he decided, in his flush of happiness about Woman, to go and buy a present for his wife.

It was market day in the town in the valley. He pottered round the antique stalls, looking at silver gravy boats and tortoiseshell snuff boxes. Nothing took his eye, so he wandered on to the livestock section of the market, where the goats and chickens were.

A chocolate coloured donkey was tied to the outside of the

goat pen. It had a white nose and stomach and white rims to the purple pools of its eyes. Its eyelashes were longer than the ones Mrs Blankenheimer had bought to go to the golf club dance, and had to trim down because they pushed her glasses off.

A small boy was sitting on the ground near the donkey, smoking a cigarette.

When Blank stopped in front of him, he squinted suspiciously up through the cigarette smoke.

'It's all right, son,' Blank said. 'I'm not going to tell you not to smoke at your age.'

'That's O.K.,' said the boy consolingly. 'You don't have to. Want to buy a donkey?'

'Not really. I just bought a horse.'

'Go on.' The boy was not interested.

'Is it your donkey?' It was a pretty, delicate thing in its smooth summer coat, the shadow of the cross over its withers, neat shell feet, dished-in face, fat enough and well cared for. Somebody's pet.

'Nah.' The boy looked at him sideways. 'I brought it down to get it sold. Belonged to my sister, see, what died. Her greatest pet it was.'

'Oh, how sad.' Tears welled into Blank's eyes. If Dora were here, she would have wanted to buy the donkey at once. 'Can't you keep it?'

'Can't afford to, because of the funeral bills, see.'

That did it. Blank handed over the price the boy asked and took the donkey's halter rope. Dora would be proud of him. He lifted the donkey into the back seat of his car, folded its legs neatly on the seat, and took it back to Follyfoot.

The donkey accepted these events calmly. It lay like a dog on the seat of the hired car, its white muzzle resting on its foreleg, regarding the passing countryside with violet eyes.

It was only when Blank was half-way up the winding hill to the farm that he remembered that he had not bought a present for his wife.

'I don't believe it.' Ron Stryker opened the back door of Blank's car. 'What makes you think we need a donkey?'

'But look at those eyes. I know Dora will be glad to have her.'

'Dora don't run this place.' Ron's eyes were sharp under the lank ginger hair. 'You'll have to take it back. The Colonel don't want another donkey.'

'But I've bought her. I can't take her back to the States. Where's Dora?'

'I dunno. She was around. Must have gone off somewhere.'

Blank left the donkey in the car and locked it, so that Ron could not play any tricks. He did not trust this sharp-tongued, red-haired boy with the wild laugh, unrecognizable as either humour or wickedness.

The day was losing its light early. The clouds were low and a damp mist had curled up from the valley to shroud the farm and fields. Blank went round the loose boxes, but there was nobody there except Woman, resting her groggy leg and too busy with her hay to greet her saviour.

He went into the tack room and called up the stairs for Steve. No answer.

'Dora!' He went down the path to the misted fields, calling for her. 'Door! Door! Door!' The rooks, swaying about in the invisible tops of the elms, gave him back, 'Door! Door!'

At last he saw her, ambling up the slope from the stream, sitting on the grey donkey, bare feet hanging, eyes half closed. Behind her, the slow movement of old horses trailed out of the mist, following the donkey, who was like a bell wether to the herd.

'I brought you a present.' Blank opened the gate.

'What is it?' Dora's eyes opened.

'That boy, the one with the red hair, he says you don't want it. It's a – it's a – well, you'll have to see.'

When each horse had turned into its own stable and dropped its head in the manger, and Dora had shut the doors on them, she went out to the car. The chocolate donkey was still meditating on the back seat.

She said at once, 'Thanks, Blank.'

'This kid's sister died, you see. It was her pet. That boy – he said you didn't want another donkey, but—'

'There's always room for one more at Follyfoot,' Dora said.

'This is such a great outfit.' Blank shook his head, smiling. 'I wish I could . . . I've got a bit of money, you know. Suppose I could start a place like this in New England, where I live. What would people think of it?'

'They'd think you were as crazy as us,' Dora laughed.

'Right now, they don't think I'm anything at all,' he said in his worst Blank nothing manner. 'But I could show 'em, couldn't I? If I did – lookit, Door – would you come out and help me get it going?'

'I couldn't, Blank. I have to work here.'

'Don't you get a vacation?'

'Well, I do, but my mother . . .' Dora had half promised her mother to go on a cultural tour of the churches of the upper Rhine.

'I'd pay your fare.'

'It's not that.' She blushed. Again money – someone else's money – was confusing things.

'You could ride my daughter's horse.' He watched her.

'Doesn't she ride it?'

'Not this year.' He looked very sad. Was the daughter dead? 'Last year she rode, but somewhere along the line, she matoored, or whatever they call it. I'd bought Robin for her. Now she won't ride him.'

'I would.'

'You would?'

'In the summer, perhaps I could come, when all the horses are out. The work's easier then.'

'In the summer.' He nodded. 'Bye, Door.'

'Bye, Blank.' Smiling, she stood with the brown donkey and watched him safely past the gatepost. It was only after his car had turned the corner that she began to get scared. Go to America? Stay with a strange family, with a mysteriously 'matoor' daughter and a father who was shyer than she was? She must be mad. She would have to get out of it somehow.

The summer was weeks away. Anything might happen before then.

eight

But nothing did happen. June drew near. Dora's passport photo looked like a wanted criminal. Blank sent over her ticket. The Colonel had agreed willingly. Steve and Callie were jealous.

Ron was fed up. The cheap horse auctions were coming up. The Colonel had that gleam in his eye. There'd be newcomers to the farm and Dora gone jet-setting across the Atlantic.

'Who's to do the work?' Ron demanded. 'Who's to do her work then?'

'It won't be you, that's certain,' Steve said.

'No, because I'll be on the Costa Brava,' Ron said. 'I'm taking me holidays in Spain.'

'You can't have no holiday,' Slugger told him.

'How can Dora then?'

'She don't miss all the work days you do.'

But Slugger was dubious about Dora's trip. All he knew of America was from television. In his mind, the United States and hell were the same place.

'But it's to help start another Follyfoot there,' Dora said. 'It's a wonderful chance. Other countries might copy it. Follyfoot International. It could be the start of a whole world movement for old horses.'

'We've lost her.' Slugger sniffed his lower lip up towards his nose. 'She's gone idealistic on us.'

'No, I haven't.' Dora dropped her starry-eyed act, which was as much to convince herself as Slugger. 'I don't really want to go.'

Dora's mother was disappointed about the Rhine cathedrals,

but she thought it would be a wonderful chance for Dora to get away from horses. Her mother had never come to terms with the turn that Dora's life had taken the day she met the Colonel and decided that her career began, and possibly ended, among the old horses of Follyfoot.

'I'm not getting away from horses,' Dora said. 'Mr Blankenheimer has a lot of them.'

'But racehorses,' her mother said. Racehorses were all right. They lived in proper stables with proper grooms, and performed a proper function in life. 'If they have a racing stable, they must be pretty grand people. You'll have to get some proper clothes.'

'Don't they wear jeans in the United States?' Dora asked.

'You're hopeless,' her mother said, and took Dora to a department store.

They bought some shorts because it was going to be hot, and a swim suit and some bright slacks and cotton dresses and one long skirt for what Dora's mother called The Evenings.

Dora was wearing a pair of heavy ankle boots with her jeans that day. The long flowered skirt looked all right until she moved. Then it looked very odd with the boots clumping about underneath.

Dora looked at herself mournfully in the unflattering mirror of the fitting room. 'I hope the days at the Blankenheimers are going to be all right,' she said dolefully, 'because I don't think I'm going to enjoy the evenings much.'

Her mother said, 'It's the chance of a lifetime.'

'Might be the end of a lifetime.' Dora had never flown before. She was afraid.

'Don't be ridiculous,' said her mother, who flew regularly to France, Italy, Germany, and didn't let on that she had a lucky charm at the bottom of her pocket. 'People fly every day.'

'But they're not scared,' Dora said, as if that were the only thing that kept them from crashing.

'Let's see if we can find a nice white frilly blouse to go with that skirt,' her mother said, to cheer her up.

'I don't think I want to go.'

On her last evening, she knew she didn't want to go.

The horses were all out in the fields. The little brown donkey with the white muzzle and endless white-tipped ears, christened Dottie, was out with Don in the summer twilight, grazing the thistles and coarse grass that the horses wouldn't touch.

'Too stupid to know good grass when they see it,' Ron said. He resented the horses for the work they made, but he resented the donkeys even more.

'Donkeys are good for a pasture, fool,' Slugger said. 'That's why we have 'em.'

'The Colonel's soft in the head, that's why we have 'em.'

They were all leaning over the gate watching the horses move away towards their night-time grazing grounds on the other side of the stream. Cobby, his chestnut coat bright in the afterglow of the sunset, swishing his thick tail like a bell. Spot the circus horse, his sagging back on which ladies had once danced showing his years. Dolly with her back feet twisting outwards, sign of an animal that has been overdriven. Magic the police horse who was so fat and well this summer that dapple marks showed on his quarters.

Woman-o'-War, with that awful dropping action of her left hind leg, but filling out already, the desperate look gone from her eye. Her roan coat was less patchy, the rubbed marks grown in, the blue colour improving as she fattened up.

Dora half closed her eyes and imagined, grazing slowly forward with the herd, her horse, her bay horse, moving easily with the long thoroughbred walk that told what his gallop would be like.

'I don't want to go,' she said.

'This time tomorrow,' Callie said, 'you'll be miles up in the air. Maybe the window will fly out, like they do sometimes, and you'll drop down, spinning like a corkscrew, and land in Nova Scotia.'

'I don't want to go.'

The Colonel took her to the airport in his rough little sports car. It was one of the few drives with him when she had not clutched the seat convulsively, and trodden on the floorboards in a desperate attempt to brake before he did. If she were killed on the road, at least she couldn't be killed in the plane.

She was very quiet.

'Excited, eh?' The Colonel turned to look at her once, saw her tight lips and turned back to the road and left her alone.

Approaching the airport, they began to see a lot of planes overhead. Dora began to get that feeling, like trying to swallow a wet stone and having it lodge somewhere between your swallow and your stomach.

'What happens,' she asked the Colonel in a small voice, 'if I'm sick on the plane?'

'You do it in a brown paper bag.'

'I haven't got a brown paper bag.'

'There'll be one in the pocket of the seat in front of you,' he said without looking at her, 'along with instructions about what to do when the plane crashes into the sea.'

'I see,' said Dora. Her hands had begun to sweat a little into the palms.

She hardly spoke. The Colonel took care of the ticket and bags, while she stood beside him, feeling smaller than usual.

When he put his hand on top of her head, she jumped. She felt extra sensitive, like a crab without its shell.

Outside the gate where she had to leave him, he started to bite his nails, because he wasn't sure whether she would want him to kiss her goodbye. She flung her arms round his neck.

'Are you sure you can manage without me?' What if they didn't notice she'd gone, and didn't care whether she ever came back?

'Of course we can't.'

'Thanks. That makes me feel much better.'

Dora walked bravely through the gate with her head up like a French aristocrat going to the guillotine.

nine

'Travelling alone?' The voice made her jump. A man had come to sit beside her on the plane. Tall. A briefcase. One of those faces that have been around. 'Bob Nelson,' he said.

She nodded. Although the plane was on the ground, she was gripping the edge of the seat as if it was in the air.

'Scared?' he asked. 'Don't be. It's boring, that's all.'

The take off was so exciting that beyond a fleeting certainty that they would hit some high tension cables, Dora forgot to be afraid. She sat by the window, saw a reservoir, saw a riding school, saw the green cabbage fields of Middlesex rushing away from her, saw Windsor Castle tilting dangerously by the narrow glittering river, and then they were into a cloud, and up beyond, where it seemed no one had ever gone before. Tall stacks of piled up brilliant white cloud, cotton wool masses, the tops of clouds where before she had seen only the leaky bottom. The sky was a piercing blue and the unseen sun a dazzling presence.

The man next to her said, 'It's fun, isn't it, seeing it for the first time?'

When you could not see the ground, there was less fear of falling on to it. Dora sat back and thought she might be enjoying it.

After lunch, she went to sleep. She woke in a panic, not knowing where she was. The plane was jolting, bumping against the clouds. It felt like that sickening moment in a car when you realize you have a flat tyre on a lonely road at night, with either no jack, or no spare tyre.

'White knuckles again.' Mr Nelson saw her gripping the seat. 'Nothing to be scared of.'

But Dora was right and he was wrong. The Captain's voice came over the intercom. 'I hate to tell you this, folks.'

Dora gripped harder.

'It's O.K.,' Mr Nelson said. 'You don't have to jump yet.'

'We have developed some small oil pipe trouble. Nothing to worry about. But in view of possible bad weather ahead, we are going to take the precaution of detouring to Keflavik, Iceland, where repairs will be effected as soon as possible.'

'I'll be God damned,' Bob Nelson said.

'Do you think I'm a jinx?'

'First time this ever happened to me.'

'Last time I'm ever going to fly,' Dora said.

They dropped down through a brilliant sky and saw the coast of Iceland like a moon landscape, bare, stony, impregnable. They flew over some scattered houses and a tiny airstrip cut perilously close to a brown rocky range of hills.

They would never make it.

'You don't have to shut your eyes.' Mr Nelson took Dora's hand.

'When you go to your execution,' she said, 'they always blindfold you.'

After the anticlimax of a smooth landing, they were taken in an ordinary bus to an ordinary hotel. They were given the same kind of dinner they might have had at London Airport. Pea soup, roast chicken and coloured ice-cream. Squares of stale bread. America was too far away. Dora would never get there.

In the morning when she looked out of her window, she knew

she was in Iceland. On the stony land behind the hotel, a herd of thick coated, shaggy ponies, with scrubby manes and long tangled tails, was nosing among the rocks, pulling at the green-grey lichen. They all looked sturdy and strong, although there didn't seem much for them to live on. At the back of the herd followed the great grandfather, grizzled nose, patchy mane, motheaten, most of his tail rubbed out at the top. He was skinny, with a combination of boniness and pot belly. A lively young pony came back to make runs and darts at him, jostling him, nipping him in the rear. The old pony stumbled and kicked out fretfully, and the young one charged him again from the other side.

Poor old fellow. In her mind, Dora put a halter on him and took him back to Follyfoot. He could be Eric the Red, after the old Icelandic adventurer.

When they took off again in the repaired plane, rising just in time over the mountains, Dora saw below them the herds of ponies dotted over the barren landscape. She leaned against the window and shut her eyes as the plane leaped upward with that powerful boost, like a good horse clearing a jump.

'I saw this old pony,' she told Bob Nelson, 'out of the hotel window.'

'You would.' She had told him about Follyfoot.

'He was old and scruffy, and the young ones were allowed to tease him because he would be dead soon. I wanted to build a crate and take him with us. He could be the first customer.'

She told him about Blank's dream of starting a Home of Rest for Horses in Elmwood, Massachusetts.

'I live near there,' he said. 'Maybe I could help.'

ten

As the plane lost height and the ground became real, Dora looked down and began to ride the countryside. So many times in a train or a car, she had ridden an imaginary course alongside, taking hedges, enormous posts and rails, iron fences, clattering down roads, leaping wide streams to keep up with herself on wheels.

Now she rode the landscape from the air, covering a hundred miles in a few minutes, galloping down a straight wide path through a forest, up a hill and down and up again through what must be a fire break, through the gardens of low houses, racing her bay thoroughbred down a grassy track between two ribbons of highway where tiny coloured cars sped nowhere in both directions.

Fear returned when they landed at Boston. Dora could not remember what Blank looked like. Would he know her in the red and white suit her mother had bought her (uncreasable) to travel in?

Coming out of the customs hall, she searched the crowd. If he wasn't there, would they deport her as an undesirable alien? She saw him, and waved, but he turned away, because it wasn't him.

'See your friend?' Bob Nelson was behind her.

'No.'

But a voice was calling, 'Door!', and there he was, smaller than she remembered, struggling towards her through the embracing, laughing, crying, exclaiming crowd – 'Hey Mom, how are ya?', 'Hi, Annie, how's my girl?', 'Oh, honey, I thought I'd never—'

'Hi, Door.'

'Hi, Blank.'

They stood and looked at each other, jostled by elbows and luggage. She had come all this way, and now there was nothing to say.

She turned to introduce Mr Nelson. 'He said he might help us with—' But before he could shake hands, Bob Nelson was pounced on by a woman and a young man, both handsome, tanned, assured, who bore him away, laughing and chattering.

'The Nelsons,' Blank said. 'They live near us.'

'You know them?'

'Everybody knows *of* them. But they wouldn't know me.'

'Oh, Blank.' Dora could talk now. 'You haven't changed a bit.'

He smiled, seeing beyond the red and white uncreasable suit and the new haircut. 'Nor have you, Door.'

'No Handle.'

Blank was proud to show Dora America. They went through an endless tunnel under the harbour, and on to a highway where four lanes of cars raced furiously. The traffic was overwhelming, but Dora was not doing the white knuckle clutch. Blank's car was so large and upholstered that it insulated you, like a tank. And she was too tired to be frightened.

'What do you think of it, huh?' Blank kept asking, but she was too tired to take much in.

At last they turned off on to a side road and drove through a lovely country of farms and fields and white wooden houses. There were quite a lot of horses. Blank showed her where the Nelsons lived, a rambling old house with a complex of stable buildings, white-railed paddocks and a riding ring.

'Wow.' Dora yawned. 'And we held hands over Iceland.'

The Blankenheimers' house was smaller, neater, the garden disciplined, chairs set formally on a stone terrace. Three cars in the shiny black drive. Were they arriving in the middle of a party? Blank stopped in front of the garage, which was a miniature replica of the house, with false upper windows and chimneys.

'Where are the horses?' Dora asked.

'My racehorses, they're at a stud in Connecticut. I've only Robin around here now. I keep him at Chuckie Fiske's stable, down the road a piece. Tremendous woman, Chuckie is. Knows it all.'

Dora had had experience with tremendous women who knew it all, and could make you feel you knew nothing, even if you knew more than they did. She was beginning to feel hopelessly tired.

Blank took her through the garage towards a door which led into the kitchen.

'Come along in,' he said. 'You're very welcome to my home.'

Dora tried to smile, but her face stretched into a tremendous yawn, like the jaw-breaking yawns of Stroller in the mornings, dribbling saliva from the vast ridged cavern of his hungry mouth. As Blank looked at her, she turned her head away to hide the yawn and yawned straight into the face of a woman coming to meet her through the kitchen.

'Hello there,' said Mrs Blankenheimer.

'Sorry,' Dora said, 'I'm terribly tired.'

'Of course you are. I know what it's like. Every time I fly the Atlantic, I just about die.'

'You only flew it once,' her husband pointed out mildly.

'And I just about died.'

She was short, like he was, a little anxious, with some bright make-up that was supposed to make her look younger, but didn't.

'I'll fix you something to eat,' she said.

'I'm not really hungry.' Dora felt rather faint.

'Of course you are. I'll fix you a stack of pancakes and some bacon.'

'No, really, I—' But Mrs Blank had headed for the stove. Dora saw that this was her style of welcome, and she had better go along with it.

She sat in a kind of booth in the kitchen, which was hung with copper pans and jelly moulds and trailing plants and ornamental notices which said things like, 'BE REASONABLE. DO IT MY WAY', and, 'ABANDON HUNGER, ALL YE WHO ENTER HERE'.

Mr Blank sat beside her with a cup of coffee.

'Can we go and see Robin after the pancakes?' Dora asked.

'Sure.'

But she did not really care about that. She suddenly felt terribly homesick. As she sat at the polished table in this clean kitchen with neat Mrs Blankenheimer making a stack of pancakes, she thought of the big round table in the messy, aromatic kitchen at Follyfoot. Anna lifting the kettle off the old stove. Callie doing homework with a fistful of bread and butter. The Colonel with one of the puppies on his lap and another asleep on his foot. Steve with his dirty boots on the bar of the table and his dark hair flopped forward over the book on genetics that he was studying for his future horse breeding career. Even the noise of Ron's motorbike starting up – the whole familiar picture swam in her head like a dream. As Mrs Blankenheimer put the plate of pancakes on the table and set the maple syrup beside it, Dora fell forward fast asleep with her hair in the butter.

eleven

She slept right through that night and half-way through the next day. Mrs Blankenheimer drove her to Blank's office so that he could take her to see Robin.

In his office, surrounded by drawing boards and bits of pipe and nails and plywood and calendars from plumbers and upholsterers, Blank seemed more at his ease. He wore stained overalls with his name Earl embroidered on the pocket, and he was called Earl by his workmen.

He took off his overalls and put on a hat – he never went anywhere without a hat – and drove Dora to Chuckie Fiske's stable. Although it was late afternoon, it was still very hot. Dora had never been so hot in her life.

The road took them between wide fields with stone walls and white fences. They stopped at an enormous barn of indoor loose boxes, with several brightly painted horse trailers in the yard. The horses were all inside. In this heat, they were kept in during the fly-pestering days. Each stall had a thick bed of clean wood shavings, an automatic watering trough, name on door, halter hanging outside.

At Follyfoot, the horses' names were on the doors, but some of them were mis-spelled, because Callie had helped to paint them two years ago when she couldn't spell. 'Lancalott'. 'Jakc and Jymmi' on the door of the box the donkey shared with the two shetlands.

Dora started writing a letter in her mind to Steve:

'*When I get back, let's smarten up the stable a bit, do some painting, get the Colonel to put in automatic watering.*'

Poor man, he could hardly afford new buckets.

They went into the tack room, where the saddles were on racks with linen covers and the bridles had not only the bits but the leather polished. Chuckie Fiske was reading a magazine, wearing cotton pants and a sleeveless shirt that showed her brawny brown arms.

'Hi,' she said without putting down the magazine.

'This is Dora,' said Blank. 'The girl I told you about, from England.'

'The one who gave you the idea about the old horses?'

'Yes,' said Dora eagerly. 'We—'

'Economically unsound,' added the woman who knew it all, 'with the price of feed and hay hitting the roof.'

Blank cleared his throat and changed the subject. 'May we go see Robin?'

'Help yourself. He's raring to go. He's short of work.'

'Can I ride him?' Dora asked. Mrs Blank had told her to come in jeans.

'Depends if you can ride or not.'

Chuckie reminded Dora of herself when she was bluntly rude to people without meaning it.

As they walked down the aisle between the loose boxes, a girl with cropped red hair pressed a switch and a cloud of insecticide came down over the backs of the horses.

'Are the flies very bad here?' Dora asked her.

'Mosquitoes too. They're a real pest. They carry the virus of encephalitis, you know?'

'I don't think we have that in England.'

'Lucky you. We're scared of another epidemic this year.'

'Here he is,' said Blank, as a bay head with a white star came over a door that said, 'King Kong'. 'Why is Robin in the wrong box?'

'That's not your horse.' The red-haired girl tried to catch

Dora's eye with a 'some people' look, but Dora wasn't having any.

Robin was in the next box. 'They are alike,' she said, although they weren't except for being bay with a white star.

King Kong was just a horse – Robin was a dream. He was part thoroughbred, part quarter horse. He had the fineness and quality of a thoroughbred, and the short back, square chest and strong quarters of the Western cattle horse. He was, like Dora's dream horse, a bright bay with a crescent-shaped star and two white feet.

He tossed his head about and his ears moved alertly back and forth every time one of the other horses snorted or banged the side of its box. But when Dora went in to him, he examined her very gently, blowing into her hand, and going over her hair with his nose to see what kind of animal she was.

He had looked a little nervous when she was standing outside the door, but a horse's expression can visibly soften when he feels reassured. Dora saw that gentle, almost smiling look in the dark blue eye that means a horse who relates well to people.

'He likes you, Door,' Blank said.

'I like him.' Dora was enchanted. All of a sudden, she wasn't homesick any more. Before, her mind had looked forward over the next three weeks, telling herself that if she could hang on for twenty-one days, it would be time to go home. Now when her mind looked forward, the date of leaving seemed like a threat, the twenty-one days not nearly long enough.

Dora went back to the tack room to get the saddle, which had a polished brass plate under the cantle saying JODY BLANK-ENHEIMER. Chuckie Fiske did not lower the magazine or take her feet off the table, but as Dora went out of the door with saddle and bridle, she said, 'Watch it, kid. He's pretty fresh.'

Dora rode by nature, not by technique. She had learned from horses, and there had not been many good ones. If she knew a horse well, she could figure out how to handle him, but she was naturally nervous with a strange horse, if she felt he knew more than she did.

Blank led her out to the gate of the white-railed riding ring as if he were leading one of his racehorses to the paddock. Two girls in shorts and pony tails who were sunning themselves in the grass, chewing gum, sat up to watch, Dora was sorry to see. She was sorrier still to see Chuckie Fiske come out of a side door of the stable and wander over to the ring.

Dora let Robin walk round the track with a loose rein. He felt edgy, very much on his toes.

'Let him walk around on a loose rein,' Chuckie ordered, as Dora came level.

'I am,' Dora muttered to Robin.

Robin's back was a bit humped. When she felt him relax, Dora let him trot on.

'Let him trot on there!' shouted Chuckie. The girls on the grass chuckled.

At the far end of the ring, a riding trail went off into the wood. A woman on a big narrow chestnut came down this trail, riding 'saddle seat', with her stirrups long and her legs stuck out. The horse was artificially showy, feet and tail carriage, exaggeratedly high. They stopped at the end of the ring and watched Dora.

Robin trotted out with easy elegance, toes just slightly turned in – that was the quarter horse in him – stride long and swinging. That was the thoroughbred. His head was set just right, the neck flexed high. He had obviously been beautifully schooled.

'Canter him!' Chuckie called.

Oh God, she couldn't make him canter. She squeezed, she sat down in the saddle. She chirruped. She said 'Canter', under her breath, in case Chuckie disapproved. She turned Robin in a small circle for the canter lead, but all he did was trot faster.

'Don't you know how to set him into a canter?' Chuckie called out.

'No,' said Dora to Robin.

She pulled him back to a walk, pretending she did not want to canter. When she got to where the woman sat on the showy chestnut, the woman said, 'Hey, you the girl from England?'

Dora pulled Robin up.

'I'll give you a tip,' the woman said. 'American horses only canter out of a walk. Pull him back. Get him on his toes. Just use your outside leg and you got it made.'

Robin stretched his neck towards the chestnut.

'Get going,' the woman said. 'She'll kill us if they squeal and strike.'

Dora walked, jogged a few collected steps, sat down in the saddle, squeezed with her outside leg, and Robin moved into the smoothest controlled canter she had ever felt. On a horse like this, she could be a good rider. She was not even aware of Chuckie leaning on the rail, of Blank with his arms folded, nodding happily, of the girls in the grass lying back again now that the fun was over.

Robin's canter was so creamy that Dora felt glued to the saddle, her torso moving rhythmically as he moved. She took him diagonally across the ring and off again in the other direction. He did a flying change of leads as if he had invented it. Dora had never ridden so well. She had never ridden a horse like this. Robin. She was in love.

twelve

That evening, Dora met Blank's daughter Jody.

She had gone up to her room to take a shower after her ride, and as so often happens in strange houses, when she came downstairs, there was nobody about. There was a smell of something in the oven, but Mrs Blank was not in the kitchen. Blank was not in his den. Neither of them was out on the terrace.

Dora wandered into the tidy living room and did a tour of the family pictures. The Blanks at their wedding, the bridegroom looking as if it were a funeral. A beautiful baby. A beautiful toddler. An eager small girl on a show pony, dressed to the teeth, rosettes on her bridle. The same girl, older, on Robin with his mane and tail plaited, also with rosettes.

'That was in the bad old days.'

The girl in the photograph had come into the room, older now, tattier, the eager look replaced by an air of disillusion, eyes heavily made up in a white face, long brown dress with the hem undone.

'I'm Jody.' She sat down and kicked off thong sandals. Her feet were as dirty as Dora's were at Follyfoot. They were clean in America, where she did not clean stables.

Ill at ease with the girl, her mind jetted back across the Atlantic and saw Steve and Slugger and Ron with the forks and barrows, mucking out.

No. If it was 8 pm here, it would be 1 am in England. The only person who could conceivably be mucking out now would be Callie, who had once got up in her sleep and been found by Steve when he came home late from a party. She was pushing a wheelbarrow in pyjamas and bare feet, her eyes fixed on nothing.

She and Jody sat on opposite sides of the room and looked at each other. They were about the same age, but there was nothing to say.

'I – er, I rode your horse today,' Dora said at last.

'Oh yeah? What d'you think of him?'

'He's fantastic. Best horse I ever rode. He's beautifully schooled. Is that your doing?'

'Somewhat, I guess. I did work on him last summer. Nothing else to do then.'

'What is there to do this summer?' Dora asked.

'I go around with this group, that's what's to do. Vince and the It. They're kinda terrific.'

'Do you mind me riding Robin?' Dora asked.

'Hell, no. Why should I care?'

'Your father said – said that it would be all right.'

'No, I mean, honest,' said Jody. 'I'm glad you came.'

'Thanks.'

'Keeps Dad happy, what the hell? Keeps him out of my hair.'

The Blanks came in from the garden where they had been picking lettuce. They had steak and salad. Dora was famished. The food was marvellous. Much too much of it. She wanted to wrap up the rest of the steak and ship it back to Steve.

'You should see how well Dora rides Robin,' Blank said.

'Oh—' Dora shot a look at Jody. 'Anyone can ride him.'

'You and Jody can. He goes well for girls. They'll miss you,' he said to his bored daughter, 'at the County Fair. First year you won't have been.'

'First year I haven't been a dumb kid, let's face it.'

'It's a pity though. All the big exhibitors will be at the Three Day Show. Good opportunity to clean up.'

'Oh Dad, for God's *sake*.'

A horn sounded outside and Jody got up and went out with a bang of the screen door.

'Why don't you let Dora show the horse, Earl, if she's so good?' Mrs Blank suggested.

'You want to, Door?' Blank's eyes were eager.

Oh no.

'Have to get Chuckie to school you a bit, of course.'

Oh *no*.

Chuckie Fiske's schooling was pretty brutal, but Dora learned a lot. She was to ride Robin in the class for Hunters under Saddle. She learned how to keep him on the rail, not get into a bunch with other horses, keep him relaxed yet moving strongly on, trot him collected, trot him extended, stop square after a hand gallop, back him straight.

Chuckie's method was short on praise and long on anguished yells. Dora was the only person who could contrive to have the perfect horse cantering on the wrong lead.

'Dorra!' shouted Chuckie. 'You British bungler! If you have to do that, for pity's sake change leads before the judge turns around and looks at you.'

'How can I tell when he's going to?'

'How can she tell?' Chuckie clutched her short grey hair and appealed to the sky. 'Anyone who isn't a total idiot can tell.'

Chuckie took Robin to the show in an enormous van with three or four of her other horses, and the gum-chewing girls who efficiently rode them.

When Dora arrived at the County Fair showgrounds with Blank, she couldn't believe her eyes. If these were the people left over after the cream had gone to the Three Day Show, what on earth must the cream look like?

She had never seen so many beautiful, well kept horses all together in one place. Robin, who was the best looking horse she had ever had any dealings with, looked unremarkable among the splendid thoroughbreds. The proud quarter horse blood which showed in his rounded quarters and crested neck and pigeon toes might be something that, if he were a person, he would want to disguise, like a thick waist or pimples.

Robin, however, was not at all crushed by such grand company. When Chuckie said, 'Throw a leg over him and work him out a bit,' Dora took him over to the edge of the showgrounds, where some girls were doing supple, minutely controlled circles and figures of eight. Robin bucked and squealed. He tossed his head, a relic of the days when he was what they called 'Western broke' in a lethal bit that punishes a horse if he tries to take hold, which is how Western horses learn to stop dead.

Dora went back to the van to put a martingale on Robin while she got him worked down to his usual controllable self.

A girl on a grey Welsh pony, serious and determined, was jumping back and forth over a bar, held by her father and an elder brother. As the pony jumped, high and neat, they raised the light bar skilfully to rap the fetlocks and make it pick up its back feet.

Dora stopped Robin to watch. The man looked round casually, then looked again and smiled.

'Hullo, there,' he said. 'I know you, don't I?' It was Bob Nelson, from the plane, the man she had been to Iceland with.

'How nice you look.' Dora was dressed in Jody's last year's breeches and jacket and boots. 'I didn't know you rode in shows.'

'I don't,' Dora said. 'It's just for fun.'

'Of course. It's no use if it isn't fun,' Mr Nelson said, his words contradicted by the fiercely determined girl, who rode up saying, 'Gee, Dad, if Colombo doesn't win, I'll kill myself.'

Her brother said to Dora, 'Nice horse that bay. Very good type.' He was a tall boy, slow and easy going, shorts and big knees and a flop of fair hair, and one of those voices that is born to have it easy. 'He certainly goes well for you.'

He grinned generously, and Dora grinned back under Jody's riding cap, flattered.

If Steve were like that, casual, assured, with one of those voices, would she like him better? On her mind's screen came a picture of her last sight of Steve going off with Dolly in the blue cart to mend fences, hair unbrushed, clothes looking as if he'd slept in them, waving goodbye to her not with a grin, but with the kind of lost, forlorn look he used to wear when he first came to Follyfoot from a life of trouble. No, she wouldn't like him better.

Watching the classes before hers, Dora became increasingly sick and nervous. If she actually threw up, would they let her miss her class? Chuckie had talked about not making a mistake in front of the judge, but the riders Dora watched did not seem to make any mistakes at all. It was hard to see how, before the end of the class, the judge eliminated some and decided who would stay to be placed.

'Come on – hurry!' Blank, in his stylish horse show suit and straw hat, called her back to the van to have Robin polished and her boots repolished, a hair net put over her protesting hair, and the number eighty-two tied round her waist. Jody's boots were too tight. Her dark blue jacket was too narrow in the shoulders. Her cap was too big, and stuffed with handkerchiefs. Dora was uncomfortable and scared. She heard Chuckie Fiske's voice calling, 'Hey, Dorra!' but paid no attention. She didn't want last minute instructions.

'The last time I'll get conned into riding in a horse show,' she told Robin as they joined the line going into the ring. It was a glorious day. The fierce heat had gone from the air. A breeze pushed small firm clouds across the very blue sky of New England. A day to be out with sandwiches in one pocket and an orange in the other, riding the hills beyond Follyfoot, with no plan at all except getting back for supper.

When she was in the ring with the other horses, Dora saw that Robin could hold his own. Some of the thoroughbreds were a bit weedy. One had a very short stride. Another poked its head. Another was being clumsily ridden by a boy who let him bend in a curve at corners.

When the loudspeaker said, 'Canter', Robin slid smoothly into his creamy canter. The brown with the blaze was on the wrong lead. Hooray. Dora prayed with fleeting spite that the judge would notice, then forgot everybody else to concentrate on showing Robin off as he deserved.

'All right, all right.' Much too soon, when she was beginning to enjoy herself, although the boots were giving her hell, the ring steward called them into the middle of the ring.

The announcer's voice came over the microphone. 'The following are excused. One hundred and twenty. Nineteen. Thirty-four. Thirty-six . . .' Confident that Robin had gone well enough to be kept back among the finalists, Dora could afford to feel sorry for those who weren't. 'One thirty eight. Eighty-two.' It was like a blow to the pit of the stomach. 'The rest of you get back out on the rail, on your left circle.'

Dora rode out of the ring at the end of the string of riders who did not seem to care. She saw Blank's disappointed face and turned the other way, saw the amiable grin of the Nelson boy, about to say 'Too bad,' swerved away and almost ran over Chuckie Fiske sitting on a camp stool drinking beer.

'It wasn't fair,' Dora said childishly. 'He went beautifully.'

'Didn't toss his head one bit did he? Maybe,' Chuckie took a long swallow of beer, and fixed Dora with an eye over the can, 'maybe that's why they don't allow martingales in showing classes.'

'Is that why I was kicked out?'

'Sure was.'

Dora remembered Chuckie calling her for last minute instructions. She pulled Robin away, went back to the van to take off his saddle and bridle and walked away with him in a halter to let him eat grass and forget.

thirteen

Dora was pretty resilient. When she was knocked down by life, she could usually find some way of bouncing herself back up again.

When she got over being angry at herself about the martingale, she bounced back with the thought that at least she could say that she could have won if she hadn't worn it, which was better than saying that she couldn't win. And she and Robin had done well, a good partnership. Only ten more days with this horse. She would ride every day and then say goodbye to him for ever and go back to Willy the mule, and tell tales about her partnership with the bay horse, which no one would quite believe.

That evening after dinner, a terrible row blazed up at the Blankenheimers' house.

Jody's boy friend Vince, of Vince and the It, was there, lounging on a terrace chair and picking skin off the soles of his feet.

Although she didn't like him, Mrs Blank was pleased that Jody and he had stayed home for dinner. She had made barbecued spare ribs and pineapple upside down cake, much too heavy and rich for this weather.

Mosquitoes were beginning to bite. 'We'll have to go indoors,' someone said, but they were too full of food to bother.

Mrs Blank got up to get the can of insecticide. She sprayed it over the remains of Jody's cake. Jody didn't want it, but she said, 'Hey, Mom, cut it out,' in her ugliest Hey Mom voice.

'You can't be too careful,' her mother fussed. 'I heard on the television that the suspected cases of encephalitis could be the start of an epidemic.'

'Scaremongering by the media,' Vince scoffed. He didn't watch television.

'What do you know about it?' Mrs Blank snapped at him.

'Don't snap at Vince,' Jody snapped at her.

'Two kids have been taken to hospital because they were bitten by mosquitoes that may have bitten infected horses. They could die, those kids.'

'Do you know 'em?' Vince asked.

'No,' Blank said. 'But they're somebody's kids, and they may be dying.'

'That's so typical of the both of you,' Jody said. 'You waste a lot of useless sentiment on a couple of strangers, and ignore what's going on with your own daughter.'

'Go on.' Vince nudged her with his big toe. 'Tell 'em.'

'It's like this, Dad,' Jody began belligerently. 'I gotta have a new car.'

'What's wrong with the VW?'

'It was O.K. once, when I was a kid, but look Dad, it's falling apart.'

'It's only a year old,' her father said mildly. 'If you'd taken a bit more care of it, remembered to put oil in once in a while—'

'I've seen this fantastic white Jaguar,' Jody said. 'I could get it on a really good trade-in for the Volks. Only need to add a couple of thousand dollars.'

'I'm sorry,' her father said. 'I don't know that we can afford that kind of thing this year.'

'I thought you were doing pretty well,' Vince said offensively. 'Putting up houses at the same cost, and raising the price of them to the customer.'

'Business isn't what it was.' Blank, who detested rows,

didn't rise to the insult. 'People haven't the money to buy and it's harder to get bank loans.'

'You bought Mom the big Buick at Christmas,' Jody said.

'Now listen here.' Her father suddenly got angry, an unusual sight, if not very terrifying. 'If I want to buy my wife a car, who's going to stop me?'

'Not I.' Jody shrugged her shoulders. 'I merely said why shouldn't you buy your daughter one too?'

Dora sat in the middle of the row uncomfortably, her head going back and forth as if she were at a tennis match. If she had talked like this to her father at home, he'd have thrown her into the street.

'And if we're so poor,' Jody persisted, 'then how come you're spending all that money on those racehorses. And how come you're pushing this crazy idea of buying a farm and filling it with old crocks, just so people will say, "Look at that noble Earl Blankenheimer"?'

'Jody, please, honey—' her mother said nervously. 'The horses are his pleasure.'

'If he'd spend a bit more on his family and a bit less on his horses . . . Chuckie is ripping you off right and left, Dad. She's always charged you too much. But even she thinks you should sell Robin.'

'Perhaps you should.' Mrs Blank was also nervous of Chuckie, who had once nearly ridden her down on a great black horse, crying, 'Get out of the way!' 'It is an unnecessary extravagance now that Jody—'

'You could get two thousand for Robin easy,' Jody said. 'Then I could have the Jag.'

'I'll never sell that horse,' Blank said. 'He means a lot to me.' He looked at Jody. 'He means to me the time when you were a happy kid, and loved the outdoors. No bitterness. Where does that bitterness come from?'

He sounded so sad, but Jody only said childishly, 'It comes from not having a Jaguar.'

Meaning well, Mrs Blank bumbled in with, 'The Nelsons would buy him, maybe. They like his looks. Dora told me. The boy, Michael, said he was a good type.'

Attacked by both his wife and daughter, Blank looked trapped. His eyes darted back and forth, seeking escape, and fastened on Dora.

'Rather than sell him,' he said, 'to the Nelsons or anyone, I'd give him away.'

'Jeez.' Vince closed his heavy-lidded eyes, and leaned back to meditate.

Dora stood up to clear plates off the table. She couldn't bear it any longer.

'People might be suspicious if you give a horse—' Mrs Blank began.

'Dora wouldn't be,' Blank said suddenly.

Dora tripped on the edge of the long skirt and dropped knives and forks on the stone terrace.

'I'll give him to Dora.'

'But what – I mean, how – I mean, I couldn't—'

'I'll fly him over to England for you. Pay his keep. I was going to make the Colonel a donation anyway.'

'Oh now, Earl—'

'But listen, Dad—'

Before Dora could answer, Blank's wife and daughter were at him. Vince woke up and said, 'Hey, lookit—'

'Yes.' Blank nodded, more confident than Dora had ever seen him. 'That's exactly what I'll do. I'll see about getting a place in a cargo plane. I'll send Robin to England for you, Door.'

Dora carried the plates out to the kitchen. Usually, she helped

Mrs Blank load them into the dishwasher. This evening, she could only leave them in the sink and go up to her room, her face on fire, her heart thudding.

She had used her last air letter. She found a postcard – a postcard, to convey earth-shaking news – and wrote to Steve:

'Back on the 15th as planned. Remember that horse I wrote to you about? Blank gave him to me. He's sending him over by air.'

Just as laconic, businesslike, as if she belonged to a world where horses flew the Atlantic every week.

'Love to everyone, wearing fur, hair, skin, feathers, scales (Callie's neglected fish). *Dora & Robin.'*

fourteen

In his bedroom over the tack room at Follyfoot, Steve was writing to Dora, on a postcard which Callie's class had sold at school last year in aid of endangered insects.

On most postcards, the picture is the best side to look at. The other side says, '*Wish you were here. Los Fritos has fantastic food. Your Dad has been a bit queer ever since we came. Don't forget to water the budgie.*'

But some postcards carry world-shaking news.

'*Dottie had a foal,*' Steve wrote. Foal? Colt? Filly? What did you call it when it was a donkey? He crossed out foal and wrote, '*Dottie had a baby. Its name is Polka Dot. Polly for short. Love, Steve.*'

Impossible to convey on a postcard the surprise of what had happened.

Dottie, the little chocolate donkey Mr Blank had bought at the market, had always been quite plump. Nobody had guessed why. Two days ago, she had begun to behave strangely. She would lie down, get up, move away from Don to another part of the field, kick out at him if he came after her, lie down again, get up, move off.

'You know what,' the Colonel said, when Steve called him out to look at Dottie. 'I think she's going into labour.'

'Shall I bring her in?'

'No, leave her out. It's warm. Leave her alone. It's best that way.'

Steve put her in a field by herself. Early the next morning, he got up and went out through the misty freshness of the new day to see how she was. At first he couldn't find her. He walked among the bushes at the bottom of the field, and then he found her by the hedge, a tiny chocolate foal in the grass, Dottie standing over it, sheltering it with her head.

In a corner of the orchard, there was a small enclosure which they had fenced in when Miss America's back was still raw, and she couldn't be turned out with another horse. Steve and Slugger got some old planks and knocked up a shed with an open doorway, so that Dottie and Polly could go in and out as they liked.

Folly, who was in the orchard with Specs, spent most of the time with his head through the fence, trying to make contact with the new phenomenon. Folly and Specs were alone in the orchard, not because the old horses bothered Folly, but because Folly was so bold and teasing that he bothered the old horses.

Polly was everybody's new mania. Callie was out there half the day playing with her, cuddling her, holding her in her lap on the grass, taking her and Dottie into the house to lie on the rug in the Colonel's study so that Anna could make a sketch of them.

Don was an outdoors donkey, but Dottie had been coming into the house ever since Blank brought her here. She had appeared at the open side door one day, questing with her white nose and violet eyes. When invited in, she lay down in front of the fire like a dog. Donkeys are naturally clean. If you don't keep one indoors more than an hour or two, you can call it house trained.

Dottie was such a calm mother, she didn't mind how many people handled her baby. Everyone was sad that Dora wasn't there to see Polly brand new like this.

'Poor old Dora.' Steve wasn't jealous of her trip to America any more. 'It's bad luck on her, missing all the fun.'

*

One day the postman came when everybody but Steve was out. He saw the red van stop in the lane, and went out to get the letters. A handful of bills, advertisements for veterinary remedies and agricultural tools, a postcard with a picture of the *Queen Elizabeth* in Boston harbour.

He turned it over. Dora had addressed it to him, although a postcard was public property.

'. . . *Remember that horse I wrote to you about? Blank gave him to me. He's sending him over by air.*'

Steve walked slowly back into the yard and sat down on the edge of the water trough to read the postcard again. It was going to take time to adjust to this before he told everybody. Dora with a horse of her own? The Dora he knew was always scrounging a ride, arguing with Callie over her right to the Cobbler, trying to get him to let her ride Miss America, waiting for Hero to be sound, making do with Willy the mule. Dora with a quarter horse-thoroughbred of her own – that would take some getting used to.

fifteen

The day that Dora got Steve's postcard with the news of the birth of the donkey foal, the younger of the children who were in hospital with encephalitis died. The other one was not expected to live.

In the western part of the state, a sixteen-year-old boy was taken to hospital with a disease of the central nervous system, suspected to be due to Eastern equine encephalitis. Doctors issued statements to say this was not true, but everyone was nervous. Newspaper, radio and television stories fanned the anxiety into a widespread encephalitis scare in New England.

Two or three horses had developed the disease and died in a few days. Horses that had been exposed to infected mosquitoes might have to be put down.

This was not in the area where Robin was, but every horse along the eastern Atlantic seaboard must have two immunization shots.

'Has Robin had his?' Dora worried.

'Oh, sure,' Blank said. 'Chuckie always sees to things like worming and shots. She knows it all.'

He and Dora went to the airport outside Boston to arrange for space in a cargo plane for Robin. There might not be a space available for some time. If a vacancy came up, they would notify Blank at once.

The countryside where the Blanks lived was gradually being swallowed by building developments and creeping suburbs. Dora and Blank had looked at some possible land for a Home of Rest, but properties with grazing space cost the earth, and people whom Blank approached for contributions had regarded him with sympathy or amused tolerance, but no direct offers of help.

Blank didn't mention it to Chuckie any more. He went to see the vet. 'How many horses have been put down this month?'

'Around thirty or forty, I think. It's getting really bad.'

'I don't mean because of the encephalitis scare. I mean because they were too old or unsound to work.'

'I could get you the figures. Dozens a month, I should say.'

'What would you think of a farm where they could be well taken care of, so they could stay alive?' Blank asked.

'Look, Mr Blankenheimer.' The vet was a sharp-featured young man with thick spectacles and a businesslike manner, more like a banker than a vet. 'This country is overrun with people *and* animals. If you ever see a paper bag in the road, in the spring, drive around it. It's likely to be full of puppies or kittens no one wants. Food supplies are getting scarcer. Pretty soon, half the population will be starving. Does it make sense to you to keep alive animals that have come to the end of their lives?'

'They've only come to the end of their lives because their owners say they have,' Dora argued. 'At Follyfoot, where we keep the old horses—'

'It may be all right in Britain,' the vet said rather patronizingly, 'but I don't see it going over here.'

Because Mr Nelson had told Dora that he might be able to help, Blank approached him about the sale of a sixty acre farm that the Nelson family owned on the side of a hill. Mr Nelson was genial about it, but still vague. The land was valuable, but he might make a fair price, as his contribution to the cause.

Give him a bit of time. He'd have to talk to agents. Blank would hear from him.

'You know what *I* hear, Earl?' Mrs Blank read all the papers and listened to all the local radio stations. 'I hear that there's a housing developer after that land, and his offer is out of sight.'

'The Nelsons wouldn't do that,' Blank said. 'They're trying to preserve this countryside, not destroy it.'

'Money talks,' Mrs Blank said sagely.

'They'd never sell to anyone like that. Not without telling me.'

'Why not? They don't care, people who have it all. Why should they?'

Mrs Blank's depressing attitudes had been undermining her husband's spirit for years. He responded much better to Dora's attitude, which was that life was good and full of hope, and he could still have as much fun as he did when he was a boy in Indiana.

'Want to climb a tree?' she asked. 'I was in the wood yesterday, and there's this tall pine with branches like a ladder. From the top, you can see all over the neighbourhood. You can see the Ellsmiths' swimming pool. Their kids are washing the dogs in it.'

'Climb a tree?' Mrs Blankenheimer said. 'At your age, Earl?'

'Come on,' he said to Dora. 'Let's go!'

From the top of the tree, you could see not only the Ellsmiths' pool, which was being ruined for swimming by the addition of a great quantity of detergent and shaggy dogs, but the flat roof of the bicycle factory where the secretaries were sunbathing in their lunch hour, and Chuckie Fiske's riding ring, where Chuckie herself was out in denims, erecting large solid fences in preparation for the jumping lesson she was going to give Dora when the sun went down.

Robin had been well schooled as a jumper, starting slow and

low and working up to heights. The trouble was that Dora had missed the starting slow bit, and was expected to be at the three foot six point where Robin was. She would prefer to wait till she got him home and start with him slow and easy over the pottery Follyfoot jumps, but Chuckie said she had her reputation to consider, and if the horse was going to England, Dora had got to be in shape to show him off properly.

In the Ellsmiths' pool, the children splashed and screamed and wrestled with the dogs. They had just been joined by a couple of ducks and the grandmother in a frilled black suit and floppy hat.

'Want to go for a swim?' she asked Blank, who was hanging grimly on to a branch below her.

The beach was about fifteen miles away. If they dawdled there, she might get back too late for her jumping lesson.

Mrs Blank had gone to a meeting of the Garden Club, where they taught plants and flowers to mind their place and be under control of the people who fed them with expensive fertilizers. Dora and Blank made sandwiches. Dora always felt rather guilty doing things in this spotless kitchen, which was a sacred place to Mrs Blank. She cleaned the stove after every meal, and never left dirty plates piled up. Dora had politely invited her to stay when she next came to England. She hoped that the state of the kitchen at Follyfoot, with its constant succession of meals and snacks, wouldn't spoil her visit.

Blank and Door found an uncrowded space at the end of the beach.

'Let's have lunch first and then swim.' Dora was starving.

'No, you have to swim before you eat.' Blank's mother had evidently given him the same orders as Dora's had. They had taken root with him, but not with her.

In her new red swim suit, she ran across the soft fine sand and plunged ecstatically into the incoming waves. This side of the

Atlantic was warmer than it ever was in England. The waves were just big enough to plunge into or dive over, or to ride on the swell with your arms out and your face to the burning sun.

She looked back to see that Blank had stayed near the edge of the sea, paddling about in the shallow water like a neat and careful dog. You almost expected to see the tip of a tail following after.

After lunch, Blank spread his beach towel out as neatly as if he were making a hospital bed, and laid himself down to sleep. He woke with a start as a large labrador jumped over his head, spattering sand in his face.

'What the—'

'Sorry!' The tall, big-jointed boy running by the water's edge looked back. 'Oh – gee, I am sorry.' He recognized Dora. It was Michael Nelson, with his sister who had ridden the grey Welsh pony at the show.

They parked their towels and snorkelling gear a little way along the beach. Dora lay down again, but she became increasingly bothered by a desire to get up and run down to the water in her new red swimsuit. And she genuinely would like another swim.

'Let's go in again.' Blank was still rubbing sand out of his eyes. 'Wash yourself off with sea water.'

'Just a quick one then. We'll have to be getting back if you're to be on time for your jumping lesson.'

The tide had gone out quite a bit. After Dora had swum some way out, her feet touched bottom and she came out on a sandbank. The water was only up to her knees. She looked back and waved at Blank, splashing about between her and the shore.

'Come on!' she called, prancing about on the sandbank. 'It's quite shallow here.' She pranced down the other side of the sandbank, and out into the deeper water.

Looking round, she saw Blank paddling towards her. She stopped swimming and lay on her back to wait for him. She was floating blissfully, watching the deepening blue of the sky as the sun dropped, and listening to the desperate cries of sea-gulls. She became aware that there was a smaller cry under the clamour of the gulls. She let down her legs and looked back. Without knowing it, she had floated away from the sandbank. Blank, trying to reach her, had stepped off the bank into the deeper water. He was floundering out of his depth, coughing and spitting and waving his arms.

At school, Dora had passed her Life Saving certificate in the public baths. Ever since, she had hoped to meet someone who was drowning, so that she could hook her arms round their shoulders and tow them safely to shore amid the cheers of the onlookers.

She yelled at Blank, 'Hang on, I'm coming!' and swam as fast as she could towards him. It took all her energies to reach him. The current that had floated her out was very strong. When she finally reached him, he was still afloat, but gasping and panicking.

He clutched at her hair, and she went under. She came up striking out, to keep him from doing it again. He clutched at her neck. 'Stop it, Blank!' She beat at his hands, but he was petrified and could not understand.

'Come on, Blank, it's Door. I'll save you. We'll do it . . . the two of us . . . Blank! No handle!' She shouted in his ear, and he relaxed a little.

She turned him on his back and swam, towing him, kicking mightily to reach the sandbank. Blank had gone limp. Small waves washed over his face. From time to time, Dora glanced round and saw in agony that she was making no headway against the current. Her muscles were so tired that all she could do was just go on kicking automatically, without conscious effort. Blank was very still and heavy. He must have passed out.

The thought came to her that he might be dead. She was so exhausted that she could think of that calmly. How would she break the news to his wife?

Swimming half in a dream, scenes drifted in and out of her head. Herself going through the house to the terrace where Mrs Blank sat with a glass of iced tea and the evening paper and the radio news. '*This afternoon, at Belair Beach . . .*' Trying to find Jody at her college. Getting Vince on the telephone. '*He's what? I can't understand you.*' Vince made a big show of not being able to understand Dora's accent. Would she have to stay for the funeral? All she wanted was to be on dry land at the top of her Follyfoot hill.

She should never have come. Never. The words matched her desperate kicks. She had known she shouldn't come. Hadn't she said so? She had thought then that it was fear of flying, but she knew now that it was a premonition of her death by drowning.

If I drown, she thought sadly, I won't be able to show Robin to Steve.

There was a splashing all round her. Arms and legs. A lot of power in the water. The Nelson boy got Blank away from her, turned him on his side with his head propped on his shoulder, and swam with a powerful stroke towards the shore. Dora, her aching arms relieved of the weight, managed to make it somehow to the sandbank. On the bank, the boy put Blank's still body on his shoulders and carried him in. Dora followed and was almost knocked down by the labrador leaping and barking at the edge of the waves.

They left Blank's car in the car park, and Michael Nelson took him and Dora home. She sat in the back with Blank wrapped in beach towels and a sailing jacket. He dozed and woke and apologized and dozed again and woke again, to murmur, 'Such a nuisance,' and fall asleep again.

Dora kept falling into an exhausted doze, from which she was woken by Elizabeth saying things like, 'It's weird that he can't swim,' and 'Didn't you know about the current on the ebb tide?' and, 'Good thing Michael and I were there.'

Once she said to Dora, 'It's a blast the way you talk. Are you from Australia or something?'

'Shut up, kid,' her brother said.

sixteen

Blank was all right, but he had to stay in bed and rest for the last few days of Dora's time in America. He wanted to get up and go to see Mr Nelson again about the sale of the farm land, but the doctor would not allow it.

Michael came to ask how he was. He sat in the kitchen with Dora and had a Coke. When she told Michael that she was leaving in two days, he said, 'What's he going to do then with that good looking bay horse, when you're not here to ride him?'

'He's giving it away.'

'Crazy waste. Who to?'

'Me. Robin's coming to England as soon as they have space on the plane.'

'Lucky,' said Michael.

The day before she was to leave, Dora went up to tell Blank that the air cargo people were on the telephone. An unexpected vacancy had come up, and Robin could fly in two days' time.

'Chuckie will take care of everything,' Blank said. 'She knows it all.'

Dora got on the bicycle and rode down to the stables. Chuckie was out in the ring, lungeing a young horse.

'Robin can fly the day after tomorrow,' Dora said. 'Could you get him to the airport?'

'No sweat,' said Chuckie.

'All his papers are in order, aren't they?' Dora asked. 'He's had his encephalitis shots, of course.'

'Dammit,' said Chuckie. She was still lungeing the young horse. Dora rotated with her in the middle of the ring. 'I was going to have the vet come next week to give the first shot to the ones who haven't had it.'

'Can't he come today? It's an emergency.'

'The horse wouldn't get the immunization certificate. He has to have two shots at an interval of ten days.'

'But Mrs Fiske!' Dora stood wringing her hands while the colt lolloped round them. 'If he doesn't get on that plane, it may be weeks before he can get another place. I want to get him on that plane so badly.'

'You and me too, babe.' Chuckie flicked the colt with the long whip. 'I want to get him out of here. I've got a year-round boarder waiting for that stall. I can't tie up space with a horse that isn't going to stay. I'm not in this business for my health, you know. Hey, Dorra, listen.' She began to haul in the colt hand over hand on the lunge rein. 'I tell you what we'll do . . .'

Next day, Mrs Blankenheimer drove Dora to the airport. Robin was to follow the next day.

When Mrs Blank came out to tell Dora it was time to leave, she was sitting with Blank on the terrace in the late afternoon sun. He was wrapped in a blanket, humped and sad.

'I will miss you, Door.'

'I can never thank you enough.'

They made rather stilted conversation, like people at railway stations, not knowing how to fill in the long goodbyes.

'You'll let me know, won't you, when you hear about the farm land,' Dora said for the tenth time.

'Yes,' said Blank for the tenth time. 'I'll let you know.'

Mrs Blank came out with the local paper. She put it on the table. Dora saw the headline of a front page story.

'NELSON FARMLAND SOLD TO DEVELOPER. CONSTRUCTION TO START SHORTLY.'

Dora picked up the paper and held it behind her back.

When she said goodbye to Blank, she said, 'And look, if you don't get that land in the end, don't worry. You'll find somewhere else just as good.'

'I don't know,' he said. 'Sometimes I wonder if there'll ever be a Follyfoot over here.'

'Of course there will.'

'I'd never do it without you.'

'I'll come back some time,' Dora said.

'Bye, Door.'

'Bye, Blank.'

She dropped the newspaper on an indoor table as they went through the house to get the car. Cowardly? Yes. But his goodbye face was bad enough without having to see it slapped by the newspaper headline.

seventeen

Steve brought the horse box to the airport, and he and Dora spent the night with a friend of his from the reform school, who was now married and living in a caravan on the edge of a muddy field.

They stayed up half the night talking. Dora was too tired and too excited to sleep. She told everything about America, as she would have to tell it again, to the Colonel and Anna and Callie and Slugger and Ron and Toby, giving different versions according to who was the audience.

In the morning, Steve couldn't start the horse box. He had left the lights on all night and the battery had run down. By the time they got to the airport, Robin had landed and been taken to the R.S.P.C.A. hostel among all the dogs, monkeys, tropical fish and pitiful plumed birds jammed side by side in travelling cages.

A girl in a blue overall with long yellow hair took them to the stable. She was about Dora's age. Lucky girl, working with such a variety of animals. As they went through a room, Dora stopped to look into a deep box full of feathers.

'Don't,' the girl said. 'It's horrible. I was so glad when you came because I was just going to have to unpack that box.'

'What's in it?'

The girl made a face. 'Hundreds of dead turkey chicks.'

Not so lucky.

Robin was in one of the big boxes at the rear of the hostel, wearing a smart blue and white summer sheet, legs wrapped in cotton wool and a new set of blue bandages, his gentle eye intelligently curious.

Dora held her hand out to him low. He dropped his nose into it, and she moved her fingers on the silky paler hair just above his nostril, his favourite place to be caressed.

Then he smelled her hair to reassure himself, and went all over Steve.

'A horse that likes the smell of people,' the blonde girl said, 'is always an easy one to handle. I wish King Kong could stay here.'

'I thought his name was Ro—' Steve began.

Dora cut in smoothly, 'That's his pet name. Isn't he great, Steve? I can't wait for you to ride him.'

Robin went into the horse box as if he had been going in and out of it all his life. All the way home, Dora had a prickly feeling in her back, knowing that he was behind her. As they came up the last bit of winding hill before the farm, she greeted each familiar tree, each bush and heap of stones, the place where Ron had skidded, showing off, and fallen off his motor bike, the hedge where Callie found the dead owl, as if she had been away for twenty years.

Callie was sitting on the wall at the side of the gate. She jumped down at once and climbed on the mudguard to look at Robin through the slats at the top of the horse box. Ron just happened to be out polishing the metal of his bike. The Colonel just happened to be crossing the yard. Slugger just happened to be painting the gate post. As the van drove through the gateway, Dora held out her hand to him.

'So she's done it again,' he said, in his Slugger way of talking at people rather than to them. 'All the way to the U-nited States, she's been, three thousand miles she's been, to bring us back another old crock.'

'Wait till you see him, Slug.' Dora let go of his hand, and they drove into the yard.

Robin seemed to be all right, apart from a slight cold and loss of appetite. Dora was suffering from jet lag too. After a few days, she rode him out to get him loosened up, and used to the new landscape.

He peered a lot at stones, and white fences, and bits of paper.

'I hope he's not going to be a shyer,' Steve said.

'He's curious.' Dora would have nothing wrong with Robin-'That's a sign of intelligence.'

They went through the wood, and decided to take the short cut home down the road, so as not to overdo Robin.

As they turned out of the narrow lane with the high hedges towards the road that ran along the top of the hills, Robin's head shot up, and a fraction of a second later, Miss America flung up her handsome narrow head. A second after that, Dora and Steve heard hoofs on the road.

They pulled in to the side. Down the hard highway, mane and stirrups flying, foam-flecked and wild-eyed, a black horse galloped frantically without a rider.

'Which way?' said Dora. 'Go to catch it, or go to see who fell off?'

'You go one way, I'll go the other.'

Steve went after the horse. Dora went on down the road. A few hundred yards farther on, she found Amanda Crowley, her doughy face distorted with tears, a painful graze reddening the side of her chin.

Dora told her to stand on a gate, and somehow got her up behind her. Robin had probably never had a doughy girl behind the saddle, but he didn't buck or fuss. Although he was so lively and responsive, he was the most unsurprised horse Dora had ever known.

Amanda had stopped bellowing and slobbering, but when Dora put her down off the horse at the back of her house, she began to weep and carry on again as she ran through the kitchen door.

Mrs Crowley came out in an apron with flour on her fore-arms.

'Can't understand it . . . gentle as a lamb, they said . . . She loves that horse like a brother . . .'

The Crowleys did not seem to have progressed much since Dopey became Woman-o'-War.

Steve trotted down the road, leading the black horse back to the Crowleys' house. Dragging it rather. It was hanging back, with its ears laid flat.

'How did you know it was theirs?' Dora went to meet him.

'It's got bits of pink ribbon tied into its mane,' he said grimly. 'Should be red. It's a tricky sort.'

'My poor baby. Poor brave little girl. Here's Rebel come back, see, safe and sound, say thank you to Steven and Doris.'

Amanda had come out again, and was snuggling and sniffing under her mother's arm.

'I didn't know you had a new horse,' Steve said. 'Where did you get him?'

'From some people Mr Crowley knows, at business. Their children have ridden him. We bought him in good faith, a real bargain and the girls have taken so much trouble over him. Can't understand . . .' The mother wiped the girl's face on her apron, rubbing the graze, and Amanda yelled and scowled and pulled away, aiming a kick at the back of her mother's solid legs.

Then she came over to the black horse and aimed a kick at him.

'Here,' said Steve. 'None of that. Was it his fault you fell off?'

'Of course it was, the pig. He pretended to be so qui – so qui – so quiet.' She started blubbering again at the memory of it. 'We were trotting along and I was singing to him, like I do, and then suddenly – he suddenly – Ow-wow-wow, it was awful, Mum!' She ran back to the apron and the floury arm.

'What then, my precious? What did that naughty horse do, and they said he was so gentle?'

'Did he shy?' Dora asked. The black horse was quiet enough now, standing with its knees slightly bent, and its large common head drooping, eyes half shut. The Crowleys certainly didn't pick horses on looks.

'Sort of, except that there was nothing to shy at.' Amanda looked out from her mother's armpit, pouting her lower lip to catch tears. 'He dropped his head suddenly and then he threw it up and hit me in the nose and sort of stood on his back legs and spun round. I didn't fall off,' she said defiantly. 'I got off. Bet you would have too.'

'Bet I would.'

Sitting on her beautiful well-behaved Robin, Dora could not help feeling sorry for the Crowleys, silly though they were, and for the bad luck they had with horses. And for the bad luck of any horse who found its way to their draughty, narrow stable in the bare paddock fenced with barbed wire.

Riding home with Steve, she was silent for a while. As they turned on to the cart track that led between the fields to the back of the farm buildings, Steve said, 'Don't bother telling me. I know what you're thinking.'

Dora sighed. 'Yes, I am. Well, why couldn't we, Steve?' She turned to him, standing sideways in her saddle. 'We've had some pretty good success with difficult horses. I know I'm not the world's greatest, but I did learn a bit about schooling from Chuckie Fiske. Rebel's not such a bad horse, in spite of that coffin head. But if he doesn't get straightened out, he'll either kill one of those girls, or they'll get rid of him and he'll be half killed by someone else who's not so soppy.'

'Now look, Dora,' Steve said. 'That's not what Follyfoot is for. We're there to look after the horses who need us. Not to take in a rogue horse who isn't worth a day's keep.'

'There's no such thing as a rogue horse,' Dora said. 'No horse is bad by nature. People make them that way, and people can cure them.'

'Don't be daft,' Steve opened the gate and let it swing back instead of holding it for Dora. 'Horses are like people. There's some will always be no good.'

Catching the gate, Dora was going to argue that too, but Steve, whose irritation with the Crowleys seemed to have seeped over on to her, turned round on Miss America's bare back and said, 'You've got one horse here already that shouldn't be here. Don't land us with another.'

'What do you mean?'

Steve kicked Miss America and trotted into the yard without answering.

'What do you *mean*?' Dora took off Robin's tack, and went into the loose box where Steve was rubbing down Miss A with an old towel, copying the Colonel's hissing whistle.

'Are you talking about Rob?'

'About the expense of him.' Steve kept his head down against the mare's side.

'Blank's paying for his keep. He'll send more next winter. He said so.'

'He also said when he was here that he'd send the Colonel a donation for the old horses. So he's sending Robin's keep instead.'

'Oh—' Dora was horrified. She hadn't seen it this way. 'Has the Colonel said this to you?'

Steve kept his head down, and went on hissing and rubbing.

eighteen

Ignoring Robin's impatient hoof against his door demanding to be let out to roll, Dora ran down the cinder path to the house, pushed past Ron inquiring, 'Where's the fire?' and Anna inquiring, 'Why haven't you put your sheets in the laundry?' and banged into the Colonel's study.

He was sitting on the rug with Dottie, the donkey foal curled up against her mother's rounded side.

Refusing to be sidetracked by this touching scene, Dora stopped with her legs apart and her arms folded and said brusquely, 'Have you and Steve been talking about me?'

'Dora, what on earth?' The Colonel looked up. The skin at the corner of his scarred eye twitched, and the other eyebrow went up. 'What are you so angry about?'

'I'm not angry. I'm upset.' That was a mild word for it. She was hurt, humiliated, shattered. She had thought everybody shared her joy in the gift of Robin. Now here they'd all been gossiping behind her back that she was taking Follyfoot money.

'Keep the money,' she told the Colonel. 'Use it to pay bills, and I'll find some way of paying for Robin. I'll get baby-sitting jobs.'

'I thought you didn't like babies.'

'I'll read to blind people.'

'There aren't any round here, except old Mr Corrigan and he can read Braille now that—'

'I'll sell something. I'll sell my clothes.'

'What clothes?'

Dora's suitcase with her dresses and long skirt and red swim suit had been lost by the airline, and Dora had not bothered to claim for it.

'I'll work for you for nothing.'

'You are, practically, the little I pay you. Dora, what on earth are we talking about?' He stroked Dottie's endless brown ears. The Colonel was the only person she would allow to touch her ears.

'You told Steve it wasn't fair of me to have Robin here.'

'Did he say that?'

Dora shook her head. Her agitation was subsiding. You could not stay agitated long in the cool, peaceful atmosphere of the Colonel's study, with two donkeys dozing.

'Who did?'

'I did.'

'Well then,' the Colonel said. 'Shut up about it, whatever it is.' He got up without disturbing the donkeys, sleeping with their long eyelashes fanned out, and went to his desk to rummage in a drawer. 'Here.' He held out a ten pound note. 'Here's a bonus to get Robin that martingale he needs. I want him to go his best here. Gives us a good name.'

Although the Colonel had sort of made things all right by not understanding what she was talking about, he still had not solved the problem, just because he didn't understand what she was talking about.

Dora would have to solve it herself.

On Sunday, when Mr Crowley would be at home, she took Robin out by himself.

'It's too hot to ride,' Steve said when he saw her mounting. A rather wet summer had steamed up into some stifling days. Nothing moved in the hot air except biting insects. Crickets in the long grass rang in your ears all afternoon.

'I'm going down to the brook to cool his legs off.'

'Hang on, then. I'll bring Hero. Do him good.'

'I'd rather go alone. I have to think.'

'See you when you come back,' Steve said cheerfully. Dora was not really speaking to him properly yet, but he had not noticed.

Callie was coming down the road on the Cobbler, bareback in shorts.

'I've been down to the stream,' she said. 'It's great. Come on, I'll go back there with you.'

'No thanks.'

Callie stuck out her tongue. 'You've got dreadfully snotty since you went to America,' she said. 'I suppose it was bound to happen.'

Dora squeezed Robin and he moved into his long, supple, pigeon-toed trot, lightly flexed, head held just right in the martingale.

Mr Crowley had changed a bit since the day of the show when he and Steve had rolled on the ground in the middle of the in-and-out. He had struck it luckier in his business and made a bit of money. When Dora offered to take Rebel for a while for the price of his grazing and a bit extra for her schooling, he agreed, encouraged by the lamentations of his women.

'You said yourself, Dad, we'd have to get rid of the horse if something wasn't done.'

'Don't sell him Daddy, don't sell Rebel. He'll be a good boy, he says he will.'

'He wants to learn.' The horse lifted a back leg sourly. 'You want to go to school, don't you, Rebel dear?'

'I'd be glad to see what I can do with him,' Dora added.

Mr Crowley, not used to offers of help in a neighbourhood where he had made no friends, agreed to let her take the horse, but no messing about and not letting them have it back when it was improved, because the girls would pine their hearts out until their black friend came back to them.

The Colonel agreed, because Dora needed the money, and because he didn't want another scene with her like the one in his study. Slugger said she would get herself killed, and Steve said he wouldn't touch the black horse with a bargepole.

But the horse seemed to be all right. Perhaps Amanda had invented the rearing and spinning story to cover up for having fallen off. Rebel performed quite steadily in the small field, trotting and cantering and hopping over low jumps. She ventured out with him and he didn't shy, although once he charged off with her when she bent forward as they pushed under a large tree. He was nervous after that. He jogged all the way home, driving Dora's brains up through the top of her perspiring head, laying his ears back at nothing.

Dora was pleased with what she had done with him, but he was still unpredictable. He was tricky in the stable. He had that funny way of laying back his ears, lowering his ugly head and lifting a back foot thoughtfully.

'She'd better not ask me to feed him on her day off,' Slugger said, watching as Dora groomed Rebel one sultry evening, avoiding his feet which stamped impatiently at flies.

'He's on grass, you know that.' Dora ducked her head as the horse's long black tail swished round and swatted her in the face.

'Good thing,' Slugger said. 'He'd be a maniac else.'

'Something not quite right.' The Colonel stood with him in the stable doorway, studying the black horse, as he and Slugger must have stood many times in their Army days, considering some military malefactor. 'Can't quite put my finger on it though, can you, Slugger?'

The old man shook his head, in the woollen hat which he still wore, even in this heat. 'It's not in me hands. It's in me head. In the eyes. In the nose.' He sniffed, scenting for trouble.

'You're always against any new horse,' Dora said. 'Rebel is all right, aren't you, sweetie?'

Sweetie swung round his head and gave her quite a hard nip. She did not allow herself to yell. As soon as Slugger and the Colonel moved on, she pulled down her shorts and saw the bruising teeth marks on her hip.

nineteen

One cooler evening, when the air was stirring at last, and free of the high whine of crickets, and the slap of hand on skin as the female mosquito stopped humming and settled to feast, Dora and Steve and Callie went out for a late ride.

Now that Steve had stopped throwing out hints about Robin, Dora was letting him ride the fine bay horse. Not because she thought it was good for Robin to be ridden by somebody else – he could happily be a one girl horse for ever – but because she wanted Steve to understand the way she felt about him. No, it wasn't that either. It was simple. She wanted Steve to enjoy what she enjoyed.

She also wanted Rebel to go well this evening, as proof of what she had accomplished. Being the perverse animal he was, he did just about everything wrong.

He kicked at Cobby while Dora was mounting, then turned and tried to brain her, going back into the stable. He struck out at one of the dogs. He pushed past Robin going through the gate. Going ahead, he humped his back and tucked in his tail and fussed about the horse behind. Following the other two he pulled and fussed and tried to run up on their tails.

He shied. He stumbled. He yawed his head about. He jogged when the others were walking. He did all the things that make a ride no fun. Steve and Callie carefully didn't criticize, and Dora set her jaw and didn't admit that she was having no fun.

She became very frustrated. When Rebel stumbled, she jerked his head up, which didn't help him to regain his footing. When he jogged, she pulled him back and tried to force him to walk. Robin and Cobby could both 'walk a hole in the wind' with their long easy stride. The farther ahead they got, the more impossible it was to make Rebel walk, since he had to jog to catch up.

When they came to a place where two tracks crossed, Dora said, 'I'm sick of this. You two go on ahead. I'm going off on my own.'

'Are you sure he—' Callie had her worried face on.

'He's all right.' Dora hauled Rebel's head round to go off at a right angle.

'Go easy with him,' Steve said. 'He's in a funny mood.'

'He's all *right*.'

He was better on his own, but he was still clumsy, dragging his toe and stumbling over stones. When his front end went down in a really devastating stumble over nothing, adrenalin rushed into Dora's system. She hauled up his head in the anger of fear, reached her hand forward and gave him a whack behind the ear.

He took off. Dora tried everything. She pulled and let go and pulled again. She crossed the reins, setting them against his neck. She leaned back and hauled. She leaned forward with her hand low on one rein and tried to turn him. She sawed, she swore. She contemplated hurling herself on to the first patch of soft ground.

They were headed for the road. Dora shut her eyes, opened them as they missed a car by yards and tore through a broken hurdle into a tussocky field dotted with trees. The horse stumbled, pecked with his nose on the ground, recovered with Dora's arms round his neck, and headed straight for a huge old tree.

It was unbelievable. It was hypnotizing. It was like those films where Japanese pilots flew down the smoke stacks of battleships. The tree was upon her, enveloped her. For the fraction of a moment, she saw every ridge of its bark, every curl of lichen, then whiteness exploded.

In her room at the farmhouse, the curtains were drawn, and Dora had finally stopped being sick. Her head was banded tight by iron, but the pills that Anna had given her were detaching her from that. The pain was there, but more observed than felt.

'How's Rebel?'

'He's all right.' Anna came to the bed. 'He cut his leg, that's all. He went after Steve and Callie. They followed his tracks back and found you. Steve wants to have him put down.'

'He's not ours.'

'He's dangerous.'

'It wasn't his fault.'

'Oh my *God*,' Anna said. 'Won't you ever grow up?'

Dora slept most of the next day in the darkened room. When she woke, it was night time, a sky brilliant with stars, a three-quarter moon making black and white patterns on the corner of the stable yard she could see from her window.

She got up and opened the door of her bedroom. All the lights were out. The clock in the hall creaked the seconds. You could only hear its feeble tick when everyone was in bed.

Dora did not want to sleep any more. She put a sweater over her pyjamas and went down to see the horses.

Robin was in the long field with most of the others. At first when she went through the gate in the moonlight, it seemed like an empty field. Then here and there shapes moved, something that had been lying down got up, grunting. Dolly appeared round a gorse bush, looked at Dora sideways, then ambled off with her hips swaying, in case Dora had come to catch her for work.

Robin materialized from somewhere, blowing down his nose. His mysterious night self that slept on grass and watched the dawn come up was remote from her. He let her put her hand on his gingery nose, but his eye stared at her instead of softening, and he suddenly swerved away and cantered off, and two or three of the other horses thudded with him out of sight below the dip of the hill.

The night was theirs. Dora felt like an intruder.

Dottie and her chocolate foal were inside the shed in their enclosure. Specs and Folly were camouflaged somewhere by shadows. In the stable, only Rebel was in a loose box, resting a puffy foreleg on the toe.

He was resting his head too. The stable had a low wooden manger at one end. Rebel's clumsy head was drooped over the bar, jaw resting on the wood.

There was something strange about his head. Dora went in to him. The moon was bright enough to see that his eye was flat and dull. His lip looked slack, a dribble of saliva damp on the wood of the manger. His neck was stretched out. He looked all ribs and belly.

When she had been in the vet's office with Blank, the vet had shown Dora a picture in *Equine Medicine and Surgery* of what a horse with Eastern equine encephalitis looked like.

It looked like Rebel.

But the virus of the disease had never been active in England. Only in America. Only in America, unless . . .

Dora slid to sit in the straw with her back to the wall and her throbbing head in her hands. The pain had come back. She couldn't think straight. But she must think. Robin . . . Chuckie . . . King Kong . . . The throbbing became the roar of Ron's motor bike as he skidded in from the road at his usual Wall of Death speed and shut off the engine. It coughed, hiccuped, and returned the night to silence.

Dora had left the door of Rebel's loose box open. Ron appeared in the moonlight, silhouetted like a space traveller in his leather clothes and helmet.

'Left me radio in the shed,' he said. 'Can't go to sleep without it, can I?'

Dora raised her head and stared at him, not understanding.

'Sitting up again then, are you?' Dora had sat up so many nights with sick horses. With Cobby, with Lancelot and Nigger, with poor old ruined Rusty, the night he died. 'Your pet lamb looks a bit rough.' He came nearer into the stable. 'I never seen a horse look like that,' he said.

'Nor have I. Except – except once in a book. Oh, Ron, I—' She dropped her head back into her hands and burst into tears. Rebel moved restlessly, shifting from foot to foot, grating his teeth on the edge of the manger.

'Here, what's this?' Ron was softer than he pretended to be. He knelt beside Dora and put his leather arm around her. 'Come on, girl, you're just weak that's all, after the concussion. You shouldn't be up. Come on, old Ronnie will take you into the house.'

'No, Ron.' She pushed him away and scrambled up, standing with her palms pressed against the wall, breathing heavily, staring in terror at the stricken horse. 'Something terrible has happened. Something has started. I can't tell anyone.'

But she had to tell someone, and so she told it to Ron. She told him about the terrible disease that could kill a horse in two or three days, and kill people too, if they were bitten by a mosquito whose saliva glands were infected by the virus. Robin's cold and 'jet lag' when he arrived could have been encephalitis, mild to him because of being immunized in other years. But mosquitoes, biting him, could have transmitted it to Rebel, to other horses, birds, rats, dogs, who in turn would infect other mosquitoes. The virus could be spreading in this neighbourhood, this county, the whole of England in the hot end of summer.

'You mean, it could be spreading to people?' Ron was still kneeling in the straw, gaping up at her, the hang of his jaw supported by the chinstrap of the helmet. 'Kids might die, like you said they did in America?'

'I don't know, Ron. I don't know. I have to think. Perhaps I'm wrong. It's too impossible. Rebel will get better, and it's all just a crazy idea. I don't know. I can't think straight any more.' She shook her head to try to clear it, and a whole Guy Fawkes' night of fireworks exploded among the nerves of her brain.

'Forget what I told you Ron – please?' She put one hand over her eyes and held the other out to him. He took it and pulled himself up. 'Don't say a word to anyone.'

'Like the grave. You know me.'

But Dora did know Ron. That was the trouble. He was the last person she should have shared her fears with. Thank God she had not told him the worst thing of all, that Robin had entered this country as King Kong, six-year-old bay with star and two white feet, the only official difference between them being that King Kong had a certificate of immunization against encephalitis and Robin did not.

The only clear thought that cut through the pain in her head was: *It's got to be kept secret.*

'Promise you won't tell.'

'One of us did ought, if it's true about the ensuffer – ensiffer – encephlawhatsit.'

'It's not. It couldn't be. Forget it.'

'Total blank.'

Ron saluted her, and shuffled his boots across the yard in dancing steps to get his radio.

Dora put a rug on the sick horse, and ministered to him as best she could.

twenty

Three o'clock in the morning was the deadest of all the dead hours on the night desk of the *Chronicle*. It was called the night desk because whoever was on duty at night sat there; but whoever was on duty during the day sat there too and answered the telephone and made notes to be written up into news stories.

Bruce Ingersoll was on the *Chronicle*'s night desk. He had only been with the local paper six months, and it was his first night duty ever, so three o'clock in the morning did not seem dead to him, but just as exciting as every hour of this first night of challenge and responsibility. The night reporter was on his own in the building. It was up to him whether the *Chronicle* missed the boat on scoops, or lived up to its local watchword of 'Always Alert'.

Bruce was like his name, a square young man with short hair, solid and eager and trustworthy. At college, he had known where he was headed. When he landed the job with the *Chronicle*, he had known that it was the first rung to Fleet Street and future glory.

The glory of a scoop could come any time. It could come tonight, although by three am it had not yet shown itself.

The night had started promisingly with a stammering small boy calling to report a fire.

'Where is it?' Bruce pulled the notepad towards him, his voice tense.

'In the grate, stupid.' Shrieks and giggles in the background.

Mr Shanker of the waterworks commission had called to render to the *Chronicle* some hot news that could not possibly wait till morning.

'Oh yes?' In spite of Mr Shanker's slow creaking voice, perhaps this was it.

It wasn't. The waterworks commission had held its ladies' night banquet at the Dog and Fox and settled the date of its annual general meeting.

'Thanks a *lot*, Mr Shanker. We're very glad to know.'

No harm in sending the poor old guy to bed feeling chuffed.

An old lady rang to say she had let out her cat at eight o'clock and he hadn't come back yet, so unlike him, naughty Tibbs. Would the *Chronicle* be sure and put an appeal in the morning edition?

The small boy again. 'There's been a murder done.'

'Where?'

'On the telly, creep.'

At two o'clock, Bruce checked the police station and received some interesting news about a five-car crash in a patch of fog on the London road. A concert pianist had broken his leg.

That's better. Bruce made himself a cup of tea, and before writing his story, he telephoned his favourite Fleet Street newspaper, where he dreamed of working some day.

'Night editor here. Five cars? Not really. We've had ten and twenty smash-ups coming in. The fog's nothing round your way. Concert pianist? Who? Who, laddie? Sorry, never heard of him.' Two other lines were ringing. 'Bye.'

Just before three, the small boy again and the giggling. Must be a pyjama party.

'Can you talk for a second?'

'Yes, but—'

'Ha, ha. Time's up.'

Bruce sighed and settled down again in the dingy room, with its long tables covered in papers and reference books, its overflowing wastepaper baskets, its grime and mess, its rusty kettle and cracked cups, which to him held the glamour of the Press.

He sat at the night desk and drank his tea and read a book called *How to Make it to the Top in Newspapers*.

The telephone rang. Perhaps this was it.

This was it.

'Listen.' The voice was urgent, conspiring. 'Listen, I gotta red hot story for you.' The accent was a little strange. It sounded at first like a disguised voice, hoarse and unfamiliar, but the story sounded genuine, and tremendous.

'There's going to be this epidemic, take a note of this. The public has got to be warned. Imported from America ... one horse dying, hundreds threatened ... the lives of thousands of 'uman beens at risk.'

'Human what?'

'Beens. People.'

'Who's this speaking?' Bruce asked for the third time.

'Doctor, er – Doctor Dillon.'

'A medical doctor?'

'Vetinery. Fully qualified vetinery doctor.'

'And where is this horse?' Bruce's pencil was racing over the notepad.

'I can't tell you where. We don't want a riot. I can tell you it's a place with a lot of horses, that's all.'

When Bruce was at school, which wasn't that long ago, he had gone on a field trip with the Natural History Class to see this place with all these old horses and some old Colonel or other who had been scared of the kids and hidden indoors. It was a ramshackle, rustic, manury place by Bruce's neat citified standards. Just the sort of place to harbour a fell disease.

'Is it Follyfoot Farm?'

'Might be. Might not. Can't tell you.'

'Dr Dillon.' Bruce's mind was working like speeding machinery on how he would handle the scoop. 'We'd like an interview.'

'With me?'

'If you agree. I'm off duty at six. Could you meet me at the stable at seven – at Follyfoot?'

'Right on.'

So it was Follyfoot. Bruce Ingersoll, ace investigator. He poured himself another cup of tea, tipped in a shot of the assistant editor's rum from the bottle behind the encyclopaedias, sat down again and pulled the telephone towards him with a happy sigh.

'Night Editor.' Same voice. A bit more tired. He had probably handled sixteen dramas from all over the world since Bruce last talked to him.

'This is the *Chronicle* again.'

'What now?' The voice was bored as well as tired.

'I've really got something for you now. Something really big. A life and death thing, it could be.'

'Shoot.'

'Well – up in the hills above this town . . .'

The phone call over, Bruce sat back in the broken swivel chair, breathed out, and patted his stomach as if he were already a Press magnate of international repute. The dingy *Chronicle* room with its filthy windows, scarred furniture and ravaged reporters' table was a huge modern office of stainless steel and glass. The gas popped under the rusty kettle. The old wood floor creaked. The plumbing knocked and groaned like corpses clamouring. But Bruce's head, as he sat back with a spreading smile, was filled with the roar of the presses, the clacking of typewriters, the ticking of tape bulletins, the sirens of motor bikes screaming in with stop press news from all the trouble centres of the world.

twenty-one

Very early in the morning, the pounding began on the door. The Colonel started awake and looked at his luminous watch. Five o'clock. He swung his feet to the floor, and searched in vain for slippers. Beside him, Anna drew the sheet up to her chin.

'Don't go down,' she murmured, still half asleep.

This old house would be easy to break into. She had always said that if thieves came, she would let them get on with it, since there was nothing worth stealing, except the Colonel's collection of horse photographs, and what thief would bother with them?

'Thieves don't knock,' the Colonel said.

The knocking was on the front door. Anyone who knew the ways of the house would come to the back door, or the side door into his study.

He went down, slid the bolt and opened the door to a small gathering of about half a dozen people waiting in the grey of dawn.

'Is this Follyfoot Farm?' The young man with crisp hair was carrying what looked like a tape recorder.

'It is, but—'

'This is where all the horses are, right? Sorry to wake you so early, sir, but this could be a big story and we want to get it into the late editions.'

'What—'

'Where's the horse?' another man asked.

'Horse? There's dozens of them.' The Colonel felt rather

cross. These people, who had presumably driven here from somewhere, were wide awake. He was still officially in the middle of his sleep.

'The one that's sick.'

'None of them is sick, as far as I know. There's one with a leg wound that was kept in last night.'

'The one that threw the girl?'

'Well, she was knocked off by a tree, if you call that thrown. How do you know about this horse?' He began to wake up.

'News story came through from a vet, it's understood.' The crisp young man with the tape recorder took a step nearer to getting into the house. 'Outbreak of encephalitis . . . the whole country threatened . . . dangerous to humans . . .'

'What on earth—?' For one desperate moment, the Colonel thought he was still asleep. He blinked hard, opened his eyes and accepted the fact that he was not.

'Come with me.'

He took them through the house and out by the back door to the stable yard towards Rebel's loose box.

The black horse was down, lying on his side, his forelegs, one bandaged, moving feebly in a kind of clawing motion. In the far corner of the box, somebody was curled up in the straw, asleep.

'Dora!'

She woke in a moment, jumped up and stood against the wall as the Colonel came in and the reporters crowded into the doorway. One of them took a flash picture. Dora flung her hand in front of her face.

The Colonel stood between Dora and the intruders.

'Did you telephone these people?' he asked.

She shook her head.

'Who then? Was it Steve?'

'He doesn't know.'

'Know what? Who does know it, whatever it is?'

'Well—' She bit her lip.

'Dora, don't be stupid. Who's responsible for this? Is it one of Ron's ridiculous games?'

'It isn't a game,' Dora whispered, looking down. 'Rebel is very ill. I saw – I talked to the vet in America about equine encephalitis. I saw some pictures. I think he's got it.'

'Encephalitis?' The Colonel said. 'I've never heard of it over here.'

'But if Robin could have carried the virus—'

'He'd be ill too. But he had his shots before he came.'

'Suppose he was infected before the shots?' Dora groped desperately for something to say. She could not tell him the truth yet.

'No, it's not possible . . .' The Colonel dropped down and put his hand on Rebel's head. 'Poor fellow. Take it easy, old man.' The horse's eyes looked dull and lifeless. 'Robin was a bit sick when he first got here, wasn't he?'

He thought for a moment, then got to his feet, took Dora out of the loose box, and shut the top and bottom doors.

'Excuse me.' He worked his way through the newspapermen.

'Just a minute, sir.'

'Excuse me. I have to call the vet.'

Woken by the noise in the yard, Steve came out of the tack room with his hair on end and found himself instantly the target of questions and speculations.

'I'm sorry,' he kept saying. 'I've no idea what you're talking about.'

'The encephalitis epidemic.'

'What do you mean?'

'You work here, don't you?'

'Yes, but I don't know anything about it, I told you.'

'This Dr Dillon says—'

'Never heard of him.' Steve set his jaw.

From the window of his cottage across the road, Slugger had seen the cars at the entrance to the farm. He ambled over, muttering to himself.

He too was pounced on. 'You work here?'

'I hope so. Unless I've been sacked overnight.'

'What do you think of all this excitement?'

'What excitement? We've had no excitement here since the badger got into the chicken run.'

He and Steve started to do their morning work. The reporters followed them round, taking pictures. Dora came up from the fields riding Robin bareback in a halter, and they took her picture too.

'The vet's on his way.' The Colonel came out of the house with Callie. 'It wasn't he who called the newspaper.'

He got Dora into an empty loose box.

'Listen,' he said to her tensely. 'It could be worse than we think. I've just checked Robin's papers again. He wasn't immunized.'

'But it's stamped, right on the papers.'

'Not for Robin. For King Kong. And they're not the same horse. It's described as two white feet, white star and snip. Robin hasn't got a white snip on his nose. You know what those swindling Yanks have done?'

He was very angry. Dora wanted to shout, 'Don't tell me – I know!' But she had to keep silent.

'They sent him over with another horse's papers. So he may not be immunized. This crazy story could be true.'

He looked at Dora fiercely. She looked into his blue outdoor eyes, but did not read suspicion there. So she kept silent.

When the vet arrived, the Colonel took him to Rebel's stable, and would not let the reporters talk to him, until he had examined Rebel and Robin.

'What do you think?' the reporters asked him. 'You want to make a statement about the danger?'

'I'm prepared to say . . .' The vet had been a country vet for many years. He had developed a way of moving and talking slowly with sick animals. A way which pleased the sick animals, but could be irritating to impatient healthy humans. 'What I think . . . I've never seen a case of, er – Eastern . . . equine . . . encephalitis.' He measured the words. 'But from my reading . . . the symptoms could suggest . . . but I, er – I, er – would never think of it if it wasn't for the horse from America. However, I've a blood sample from both horses, of course. Tests on mice . . . Time to develop . . . There's nowhere round here equipped to do the tests. I'll be driving them up to London.'

'I'll be glad to run them up there for you.' The crisp young man had seen the vet's muddy old car, and could guess at his driving speed.

'Thank you. It's my responsibility.'

The vet chugged off in his old workhorse of a car.

'That's about it then,' the BBC man said. 'Can we use your telephone, Colonel?'

'No.'

'Why not, sir?'

Callie took a look at the Colonel and saw that he was near the breaking point.

'Because I just cut the wires,' she said, took the Colonel indoors and slammed the door.

The reporters went up to the village and knocked on the door of the Three Horseshoes. The little pub had not had so many people in it since Bank Holiday. It was not opening time, but Toby's father gave everyone free beer, since fame had come to the village.

twenty-two

By the next day, the news had spread. The stories in the papers were mostly speculation, but it was enough to start wild rumours all over the country of an outbreak dangerous to humans.

Spokesmen from across the Atlantic were heard on the radio talking about the epidemic in New England. A child was admitted to a Midland hospital with a fever of unknown origin. Straight away the cry went up that the epidemic had indeed begun.

Some people from the Royal Veterinary College drove a horse ambulance into the stable yard, somehow got a sling under poor old Rebel, hauled him into the ambulance and took him away.

His loose box was closed up, with a sign on the door saying 'Keep Out'. Callie, who had recently done the history of the Great Plague, painted a cross on the door as they did in 1665 on stricken houses. Dora just caught her in time to stop her adding, 'Lord have mercy on us.'

Reporters came constantly to the farm, including an eager young man from the local paper who claimed to have been the person contacted by the mysterious Dr Dillon. He was crushed to find the good Doctor not available.

'He promised me an exclusive interview.'

'Very exclusive, it would be,' the Colonel said grimly, shepherding him out of his study, 'since as far as we know, he doesn't exist.'

The reporters hung about the yard in the sun, watching rather cynically as Dora and Steve went about their work.

When Steve went into Woman's stable with a bowl of feed, and Dora followed with a wheelbarrow and shovel, one of the newspapermen was heard to sing casually:

'Will you take this advice I hand you like a brother?
Or are you not seeing things too clear?
Are you too much in love to hear?
Is it all going in one end and out the other?'

Slugger had his photograph taken in various poses. Robin, who was quarantined in the foaling stable, had a picture of his head looking over the door taken with a long range camera. It appeared in the evening papers captioned: 'UNWELCOME IMMIGRANT'.

Ron had not turned up for work. That was nothing unusual. Dora was thankful that he was out of her way. Shocked and appalled at what was happening, she could not face admitting that it was she who had broken the news.

After the brief rain, the hot weather had returned. Since there was a greater risk of a horse being bitten by a mosquito out of doors, people in the area were urged to keep their horses and ponies in at night. All the Follyfoot horses were in, of course, fretting to be out in the fields, banging on doors, calling for attention every time someone they knew came into the yard. Having them all stabled made ten times the work, and the intruders didn't help. The Colonel got his friend, a retired policeman, to sit on a stool by the gate and keep all visitors out. Being deaf and not understanding their involvement, he was rude to the Crowleys, and they went away, adding the insult to the long list they felt that life had handed them.

twenty-three

Geoffrey Masters got pretty fed up with his parents always going out at night.

They were rather young to have a boy of ten years old, especially a very bright boy who read all the magazines they left lying about and watched television programmes meant for grown-ups when his parents were out.

When he said to them, 'Family life in Britain is dying and people like you are the cause of it,' they laughed good naturedly and ruffled his thatch of orange coloured hair – he hated the ruffling and the colour – and said that he should be proud to have parents who were not fuddy-duddies. When he complained about having to take off his shoes before stepping on the white carpet or not being allowed to have his cat in the house because it jumped on the dresser, his mother, who collected the kind of useless china that was too expensive to eat off, said, 'Some day you'll be proud to have been brought up in a house with such nice things.'

He was not proud yet.

His father's mother, Grandma Masters, who was quite unmasterful, lived with them in a room of her own surrounded by every present anyone had ever given her, and family pictures. Some of the old ones of his father looked like Geoffrey did now. Red hair and freckles, knock knees and long thin feet.

'Yes, my dear,' Grandma Masters was fond of saying. 'You've got your father's knees, that's for sure. And that's a funny thing,' she added. 'Considering how much time you spend on that pony of yours, a person would expect you to be bow-legged.'

Geoffrey's pony was the most important thing in his life. His parents did not usually give him what he needed, since their idea of what a ten-year-old boy needed was different from his. But they had surprised him on his last birthday with Archibald.

He had not known he wanted a pony, but when he saw this one, staked out on the back lawn eating the good clover grass, his heart rushed out to it and he knew that this was what had been lacking from his life.

Archibald was a fine Dartmoor pony, glossy brown like conkers. His mane could not decide which side to lie on, so favoured both, with a parting in the middle. He had a long thick tail, which Geoffrey brushed and combed every day, and tied up in a knot when it was muddy.

This winter, when the tennis club was closed and the Sunday barbecue parties finished, his Dad was going to take some week-ends off from the social round and build a little stable for Archie. Meanwhile, he stayed out in the small field behind the house and sheltered under the chestnut tree in the hot sun or the night-time rain.

Geoffrey sometimes read bits of the evening paper to his grandmother after his parents had gone out. He read to her that everyone had been warned to keep their horses in at night because of the epidemic scare.

'That's all very well for those who have a stable,' he said.

'Archibald will be all right,' Grandma said. 'It's only a stupid scare.'

'That's what you said about the building that collapsed in Rochester.' Geoffrey was up with all the news. 'That's what you said about the lead in paint being dangerous to babies.'

Grandma closed her eyes. Geoffrey was about to give her a lecture.

'That's what you said when I told you they were going to make the sweetshop into a supermarket.'

'Don't you worry, dear.' She opened her eyes and turned them back to the television. He kissed her and went out. She was a decent enough grandmother, but no good for conversation.

He went out to talk to Archie in the muggy night, full of the vibrations of insects. Fireflies glinted in the hedge. Geoffrey hung his arms over Archie's back, which was just the right height for hanging your arms over and resting your chin on and thinking. A mosquito bit him on the forehead.

That did it. 'Come on, Arch,' he said. 'If I lose you, I'll lose the best friend a boy ever had.'

He unclipped the halter rope and led him towards the house.

Grandma's room was at the front. At the back of the kitchen, there was a little kind of pantry cupboard where Geoffrey's mother kept flower vases and some of the china that was too expensive to eat off. The only way to get to it was through the kitchen.

Archie didn't want to come in, so Geoffrey put some sugar in the palm of his hand and walked ahead of him, holding out his hand.

Geoffrey managed to get him through the kitchen without too much damage. His long tail knocked down the salt and pepper shakers that were shaped like owls. Good thing it wasn't the ones that were shaped like swans, with breakable necks.

He took the pony round the table and into the pantry. Archie just fitted in there. He stood quite contentedly. It was stifling hot though, so Geoffrey squeezed past him to open the bottom of the window, squeezed back to tie his tail in a knot so that he wouldn't whisk it around the shelves, and went upstairs to bed to read by the light of a torch. His mother had taken the bulb out of his lamp, so that he couldn't read.

At two o'clock in the morning, Mr and Mrs Masters were quarrelling on their way home from the party.

'I'm sick of you always imagining things,' he said.

'I didn't imagine that woman insulting me. Oh! Be careful, Roderick. There's a rabbit in the road.'

'It's a stone, you idiot. Get your eyes examined.'

As they went past the row of cottages at Upham's Corner, she said, 'I smell smoke. We should stop and ring up the fire station.'

Further on, she saw a cat up a tree and wanted Mr Masters to stop the car and climb up after it. Nearer home, seeing a man walking back from a date with his girl, she said, 'I don't recognize him. He could be a prowler. Let's ring the police.'

Roderick got pretty sick of her fancies. He did not pay much attention. As they went past the house to the gate of the drive, she gave a little scream.

'What now?'

She clutched his arm and he almost scraped the gatepost.

'There's a horse's head sticking out of the window.'

'It's not your eyes that want examining. It's your head,' he grumbled. 'Get up to bed. You'll feel better in the morning.'

In the morning, when she came down in her black silk kimono with the red poppies, she didn't feel better, she felt worse.

'Archibald is in the pantry with all my good china.' She woke up Geoffrey.

'Because of the mosquitoes, you see.'

She didn't want an explanation. 'How will we get him out of there without breaking something?'

Geoffrey got up and went down. He took hold of Archie's thick knotted tail and pulled backwards. The pony came out like a cork from a bottle. He only broke one Wedgwood jug and a Rockingham saucer. Geoffrey's mother went to wake up his father.

Geoffrey's father cancelled a tennis match and a cocktail party, and spent the day beginning the work on the stable for Archibald.

twenty-four

There was another boy who had a pony in that neighbourhood, and he had no stable for it either. He only had it on loan for the summer, and a neighbour allowed him to graze it in his field, along with some cows.

On the local radio news, it didn't say anything about cows. It said horses and ponies. It said Grave Danger and Mosquito-borne Virus. It said (or hinted) that anyone who cared at all about their horse or pony would keep it under cover where there was less danger of getting bitten.

This boy whose name was Rubin did not actually care much about the pony. He had not been able to tell anyone that, however, since most of the children in his neighbourhood were either pony-mad or pony-hungry. They either rode all the time, or wished they could. It was a pity that the family who had lent him this pony had not lent it to one of the pony-hungry people. But Rubin had been in a lot of trouble this year, both at school and at home, and they thought that a nice wholesome summer with a fat grey pony would show him a Good Way of Life.

Rubin's idea of the good life was to hang around with his mates down by the canal. His mates were not the kind who had ponies, or wanted them. In their busy lives of knocking things off from Woolworth's and the market stalls and trading the items for cash, smashing things that annoyed them, like windshields, and sitting on the canal wall smoking and planning the next project, there was no time for such childish things.

Rubin had not told them about the grey pony. He had not

told his parents that he was still seeing his mates. Since he rode the pony out almost every day, they thought he was getting wholesome. They did not know that he rode towards town, tied the pony up in the tumbledown shed behind Carter's coal yard, and sneaked between the buildings and down the alley to the yard where his mates gathered to pass round the cigarettes nicked from a table in the caff last night and discuss new ways of destroying the plumbing in the gents at the cinema.

But when he heard the radio warning, he did confide in his best friend Arthur, who had been in so many tight places that he knew how to keep his mouth shut.

'If that pony kicks the bucket, you see,' he told Arthur, 'I'll have no cover story. They think I go riding all day. If there's no pony, they'll never let me go off on my own, and I'll miss the big thing at the warehouse.'

'You got no shed, not nothing, at your place?' Arthur asked.

'Only the garage, and that's got my father's car in it.'

Rubin and his father did not get along very well, so he spoke of him as My Father to make up for feeling sometimes that he didn't have a father.

'It's mostly nights they said was the danger time, right?'

'And that's just the time the car is always in the garage.'

'And just the time your dear old Dad will be tucked up in bed o-blivious, right?'

'Right.'

Late that night, Arthur sneaked down to Rubin's house. He waited by the garage until Rubin came out and said, 'My father's in bed and asleep.'

They opened the garage door cautiously. Rubin could not drive, so Arthur, who said he could, was the one who backed the car out.

He put it into forward gear first, and smashed the headlamps against the workbench. Because he knew how to drive, he was able to get it into reverse. He backed out fast, just missing Rubin who was holding the door, couldn't reach the footbrake, couldn't find the handbrake, and crashed through a fence with a night-shattering noise of breaking glass and splintering wood. He stopped with his back wheels against the next door garage, opened the door and ran.

When Rubin's father came out, it was obvious what Rubin had done. He tried to explain about the pony, but his father had heard enough of Rubin's stories to know a fairytale excuse when he heard one. Rubin was confined to the house and garden for the rest of the holidays. He missed the raid on the warehouse, and so missed being picked up with Arthur and the rest by the police car which was waiting for them outside the broken window.

The grey pony went back to its owners. They were very disappointed with Rubin for not having found a Good Way of Life.

There were also three girls who had a pony, which could not be brought in at night because there was no place to keep it.

Yes there was. It was a very small pony, not much bigger than a shetland. On the day that the Royal Veterinary College sent out its warning to horse owners, there was parked outside the house where the girls lived a closed grey van of the kind used by the plumbers and painters to carry their equipment. It had been there for days. On its sides was painted, 'J.E. DUGGAN. HOME REPAIRS ALL SORTS. DECORATIONS. GUTTERS. UPHOLSTERING. U NAME IT.' The van was empty. The girls knew that, because the back door was unlocked and they had looked.

So when the warning came, it was obvious where they could store the pony out of danger. It was a lot of trouble to get it into the van, but with one of them getting her shoulders under the front end, and the other two lifting a back leg each, they finally got their beloved pet into the van, closed the door and went to bed relieved that Ponto was safe from harm for tonight at least.

Early the next morning, J. E. Duggan, who had run out of petrol and taken a bus into town, came back with a can. He put a gallon in the tank, filled up at a service station, and drove on back to Scotland with the pony.

Those were only a few of the things that happened that night of the Great Encephalitis Epidemic Scare.

twenty-five

Another thing that happened that night was that Callie found Dora crying in the tack room, wiping her eyes with a grubby rag that had last been used to polish a snaffle.

'Oh come on.' Callie quite often cried herself, but it unnerved her to see a grown-up doing it. 'Robin's all right, and if Rebel dies – well, he might never have been rideable anyway. Steve says he would have killed somebody in the end, and you'd have been lucky if it was one of the Crowleys and not you.'

'Steve says.' Dora sighed and twisted the rag in her hands. 'Steve is always saying. He knows it all. Like—' she made a sound between a laugh and a sob – 'like Chuckie Fiske.'

'Who's she? Oh, I remember. The one who said you were the only idiot in the world who could get Robin on the wrong lead.' Callie had heard the saga of America many times. 'Chuckie Fiske, she knows it all.'

'She knows nothing,' Dora said bitterly. 'It's all her fault.'

'What is?'

'Steve told me that if the disease is confirmed, all our horses here will probably have to be put down.'

All our horses here? Callie stared at Dora. She felt that the blood had dropped from her face into a pool of lead in her stomach. All our horses – Cobby? Hero? Specs and Folly? Lancelot who had survived so stubbornly?

Dora was sitting on the broken chair, staring blankly at a five-year old calendar on the wall from E. Tibbets, Grain and Hay. Callie ran out.

She went to bed early, without supper. She didn't want to

see anyone. She lay upstairs and listened to voices, the phone ringing, feet running. It seemed for ever before the house finally settled down for the night.

Long after everyone was asleep, Callie was still keeping herself awake by pinching bits of skin, scratching her toenails against her ankles, reciting dates of Kings and Queens and finding towns and rivers and colours and trees and types of horse for all the letters of the alphabet.

Through her open window, she could hear the stabled horses stamping and snorting. In the winter, they mostly lay down quietly. Now they could not get used to the loss of their summer freedom. When Callie leaned out of the window and said 'Cobby,' he heard her at once and answered.

She dressed again and went downstairs. The friendly house was still and unfamiliar, full of strange creaks and knocks and angled moonlit patches. The Colonel's dog stirred and thumped her tail. The cats sleeping on piles of laundry and newspapers took no notice as Callie let herself quietly out of the back door and went to the stables.

One by one, she led the horses out to the big field and turned them loose. Cobbler's Dream was last, and the grey donkey. Riding Cobby and leading Donald, she went down the grass track into the field and shut the gate behind her.

Dottie, watching from the orchard, brayed a strangled question.

'Shut up,' Callie told her. 'You'll have to stay and risk it.' Polly was too little to let loose with the others.

She rode among the horses, still leading the grey donkey, down the hill, across the bridge over the stream, and out to the far end of the long pasture, where the grass became harsher and the bushes thicker as the land approached the open moorland beyond the farm boundaries.

The old horses were in the habit of following Don, and they followed him now, straggling in singles and groups, pausing at the open gate, and then following Callie on through, cautiously scenting the wide spaces that were not fenced or hedged.

Callie got off, removed the donkey's halter, and threw some pebbles at him to make him run ahead. The horses followed. When they were all through the gate, she shut it behind them. With her face set as a stone and her heart numb with loss, she slipped off Cobby's halter, and without looking back at her, he trotted after the rest of the other horses over the dipping moorland.

twenty-six

Ron Stryker felt deprived. Cheated of glory.

It was he who had made the historic telephone call, awakening the nation to the threat of an epidemic. Now everyone but him was getting the publicity. Everyone but poor old Dr Dillon.

He couldn't go to the farm to give newsmen the chance of a picture of the Man who Broke the News, because the Colonel would get after him with an iron rake for doing the Dr Dillon act, so he decided to go to London and let one of the big dailies have an Exclusive.

His motor bike was not licensed for this quarter. That was all right for buzzing round the local roads where the police were dozy, but a trip to London was too risky. Ron got out on the main road and started using his thumb.

Expert at the art he was, never failed to get a lift. Looks and personality, that's what did it.

Looks and personality kept him walking for about half an hour, while cars whizzed uncaring by him. Then a car going fast slowed ahead of him and pulled to the side of the road. Ron panted to catch up with it.

The driver was lighting a cigarette.

'Thanks for stopping for me.' Ron opened the door.

'I didn't,' the driver said. 'I stopped to get a packet of cigarettes out of my coat.'

'My mistake.' Ron was going to shut the door, but the man said indifferently, 'Get in anyway. It doesn't matter.'

'Going to London?' Ron asked. The man nodded and Ron hugged himself. Never failed. Always the old luck.

'I'm going to Fleet Street,' he said, 'as a matter of fact.'

Since the driver appeared unmoved, he added, 'Exclusive story on the big horse disease epidemic. They want pictures of the man who broke the news.'

'That rather suspicious sounding vet?' the driver asked. 'I'm a doctor myself, so naturally I was interested, but those first reports sounded a bit whacky.'

'Bad reporting,' Ron said. But he decided to settle for being Dr Dillon's assistant, rather than whacky Dr Dillon.

'You're a vet's assistant?' The doctor's glance took in Ron's tangled red hair, his leather jacket with the oil marks, the tattoo on the back of his right hand which said 'Rita'.

'Yerss, and so naturally I've been involved in the whole affair.' Ron had many accents available for use. This one was taken from the Colonel's friend Sir Richard Wortley, who had a strawberry nose, and pointed at old horses with his stick and said, 'Getting a bit groggy on his pins, what?'

'What is your estimate then,' the doctor inquired politely, 'of the biological factors favourable for the perpetuation of the virus through infected vertebrates?'

'Do what?'

'Next question: what's the point of trying to put me on?'

'Well—' Ron shifted uneasily. 'Just having a bit of a lark.'

'I don't like people having larks in my car.' The doctor stopped, leaned across and opened the door. Ron got out and gave a cheery wave, to show he didn't mind bad manners.

The next car that stopped was driven by a simple looking boy, with a thatch of pale yellow hair and a crop of fiery pimples. Who should Ron be this time? The boy looked impressionable. He might do his pop singer bit.

When the boy asked, 'Going to London?' Ron said, 'Yes. Got a couple of concerts booked. I always travel this way because I like to meet my fans.'

'Who are you then?' The boy turned on him a vacant gape.

'Silk Valliant.' Ron studied his long dirty nails.

'Silk Valliant!' the boy mooed, disguising by over-enthusiasm the fact that he had never heard of him. 'Wow, wait till I tell the gang I gave a lift to Silk Valliant. I do a bit with the drums myself,' he added modestly, 'but of course, not in your class.'

'Ah well.' Silk Valliant settled back and prepared to enjoy the drive. 'We've all got to start somewhere.'

When the boy stopped to let him out at that point where he turned off the London road, Ron fished in his pocket and put two green tickets into the glove compartment.

'Tickets for my concert,' he said. 'Bring your old lady. Come round and see me after.'

'Gosh, thanks.' The boy's bumpy skin flamed. After he had driven on alone for a while, he took out the tickets. They said, 'Parish Church of Ashbury serving Little Moulsden. Summer Fayre. Grand Raffle. First Prize a 14 lb Goose.'

Nobody stopped for Ron for a long time. He sat by the side of the road and rubbed his ankle, with an expression of pain that people were going too fast to notice, even if they cared. The only person who cared was a little old lady going slow enough to notice. She stopped and backed up to him fast, almost running over the leg he wasn't rubbing.

'Do you need to go to a hospital?' she asked hopefully.

'No,' said Ron. 'I've had that bullet in there so long, they reckon they'll leave it.'

He got into the car, and almost immediately regretted it. The lady pulled across to the middle lane and drove at thirty miles an hour, with people passing her on both sides. From time to time, she wobbled off course. Drivers hooted, glared and shook their fists. Children jeered through back windows. Ron slumped in his seat, hoping not to be seen.

'Are you all right?' the old lady asked sunnily. 'You look deathly pale.'

'Please stop the car and put me out,' Ron said faintly. 'I think I'm going to be car sick.'

'Oh, we can take care of that, my dear.' She pulled out some paper bags from under the seat. 'I've got a little grandson who always throws up, so I'm prepared. Goodness, that lorry came close to me.' She had wavered almost into the path of a big lorry, which had swerved just in time, stark horror on the driver's face.

'Let me out,' Ron begged.

'I said I'd take you all the way into London. Don't thank me. I like the company.'

'I've got smallpox,' Ron said, but a car was hooting at her and she didn't hear. He prayed for a quick death, but a busy roundabout came instead. The old lady had to slow. He opened the door, jumped and ran.

He was taken on into London in a van driven by an old mate of his. Ron didn't have to put on an act for him, so he told him the story about the sick horse and his phone call and how it had started this whole hullabaloo.

The mate didn't read the newspapers, except for the sports pages, and he only listened to rock music on radio, so this was the first he'd heard of it.

'Go on,' he said. 'You must think I was born yesterday, Ronald Stryker. What a pack of lies.'

'Now it's funny you should say that,' Ron said, 'because for the first time in me life, I'm telling you the clean, unvarnished truth.'

*

When he got to the office of the newspaper he had picked to favour with his Exclusive Story, the doorman would not let him go up to the news room.

'Bomb scares,' he said. 'Sorry. State your business and I'll send up a message.'

'I'm the one who broke the news about the epidemic of ephalitis – elephantisis – you know. Dr Dillon. I've come to have me picture taken.'

The doorman spoke on the telephone.

'I'm sorry,' he said more firmly. 'There's no one up there able to see you.'

'But they must,' cried Ron. 'They're daft, they don't know their business.' There were people going in and out of the lifts all the time. This made him furious. 'It's hot news. Call back again.'

'I'm sorry.'

'Don't keep *saying* that.'

Ron was so frustrated that he set fire to the wastepaper basket (give 'em some hot news). The doorman smothered the fire, sighed and called upstairs for someone to come and deal with Dr Dillon.

A girl came down. They sent a mere girl, who looked as if it was her first day on the job.

'What is it that you want?'

'It's about the great epidemic, innit?'

'What great epidemic?' the girl asked. 'There never was one.'

'There was too. You don't know your job, mate. There's the great horse epidemic. All kids in Britain threatened. Never been a story like it.'

'Never been a flop like it.' The girl laughed. 'Haven't you heard the news?'

'What news? I been on the road since morning.'

'That horse died.'

'There you are, what did I tell you?'

'They cut it open. What do you think it died of?'

'What I said – elphlacitis – elepan—'

'It died of a brain tumour. There's no epidemic.'

'But I come all the way to London!'

'Sorry about that.' She got him firmly to the door and out into the street. All right, so it wasn't her first day on the job.

Ron felt very discouraged and quite fagged out. He went to see an acquaintance of his who sold souvenirs in Oxford Street, borrowed some money, and went back by train.

His way home from the station to the cottage where he lived with his mother took him past Follyfoot. He looked across the field at the top of the hill, where lights and shadows moved across the grass in a pattern of moon and clouds. Someone was coming up the long slope. A poacher? If it was old Bob, he owed Ron five pounds.

Ron climbed the gate and stood behind a tree. It was a very small poacher. It was Callie.

'Ron!' She gasped and jumped as he stepped out in front of her.

'Been courting, dear?'

He saw that her face was streaked with tears and dust, and that her breath was coming in hard, dry sobs.

'What's up?'

'Oh Ron, it's awful.' She raised her face to his and tears began to run again down the tracks the others had made. 'Oh Ron—'

'Oh Ron what?'

'It's—' She took a deep breath and swallowed. 'It's one of the puppies. The one with the bent tail. He's been missing since morning and I can't find him anywhere.'

'Them pups is old enough to take care of themselves.' Ron put an arm round her. 'Never you mind, love. You go on to bed, and we'll have a good look in the morning.'

'All right,' she whispered. She was as white as a little ghost. Ron would have liked to tell her about his horrible day, but he hadn't the heart. He'd tell his mother and his mother would say, 'Trouble? You don't know the meaning of the word if you've not lived with this pain I suffer in my back, night and day . . .'

He walked with Callie to the gate that led to the stables, boosted her over it, and watched her run like a thin scared animal across the yard and into the house.

twenty-seven

Callie dozed and woke and dropped into a nightmare of charging horses from which she woke with a cry and an arm flung over her face, in fear of being trampled. She had hoped to sleep most of the next day, because she did not want to face the next day, but the mercy of sleep was denied her. She lay scared and trembling, chewing on the sheet, her eyes staring into the gradually spreading light.

When she could stand it no longer, she gave a deep sigh, stepped into last night's clothes in a heap by the bed and started downstairs. Someone was frying already.

In the kitchen, Dora was scooping out of a pan three fried eggs with burned bottoms and broken yolks.

'Want me to do you some, Cal?'

Dora looked unnervingly bright and healthy compared to the way Callie felt after her night of tears and nightmare. Callie shook her head. She poured herself a mug of tea from the enormous potful that Dora had made, and sat down at the table, cradling the steaming mug moodily in her hands.

'Pig, aren't I?' Dora had started on the eggs and a hunk of bread and butter. 'I always say it should be horses first, then people, but this morning, I felt like feeding myself first before our four-legged friends out there.'

She didn't know yet.

'I was starving.' Dora sopped bread in the greasy eggs. 'Must be the relief.'

In Callie's miserable, sleep-starved brain, a thought began to register. It finally became clear.

'Relief?' She looked up.

'That's right.' Dora put down her knife and fork. 'Good Lord, nobody's told you yet. You went to bed so early yesterday, you were asleep when the fantastic news came through.'

'What news?' No news could be fantastic at this point.

'About Rebel. He died, you know. Not that that's fantastic, but well – the poor thing was dying anyway. The thing is, what he died of. The tests on the mice still weren't confirmed, but as soon as he died, they did a post mortem, and what do you think they found?'

'Massive brain damage due to the virus,' Callie growled. She knew what encephalitis could do.

'A tumour. A brain tumour. Not that big, but in a vulnerable spot. It would account for the erratic way he behaved, if a branch knocked him, or some fool like me hit him behind the ear. So Robin's in the clear. The scare's off.'

Callie stood up and turned away from her grin. She went to stand by the window. She was going to have to speak without looking at Dora.

'We should have woken you, I suppose,' Dora went on. 'But you looked so peaceful.' Callie's faking face, that must have been, with her arms crossed over her chest like a dead maiden, lacking only a lily between her hands.

'I feel so good, I've half a mind to fry myself another egg. Are you sure you—'

'Dora,' Callie said in a hollow voice. 'Last night, in the middle of the night, I got up.'

'Why?' Dora was at the stove. She cracked one of the big brown eggs that Henrietta laid in Wonderboy's hay rack (he preferred his hay off the floor anyway) and dropped it into the pan.

'You told me that the Follyfoot horses might have to be destroyed.'

'That's what they thought then. It was unbearable. I never want to have to go through another day like that again.'

'This one isn't going to be too good,' Callie said in a small voice. 'I thought – you see, I thought they were going to shoot all our horses, so I took them down to the end of the long field and let them out on to the moor.'

'You *what*?' Dora was concentrating on getting the egg out of the pan, only half hearing.

'I did. I let them all out on to the moor. They followed the donkey.'

'Including Robin?' Dora turned round with the plate in one hand and the spatula in the other.

Callie nodded.

'Stupid idiot!' Callie had never seen Dora so angry. Dumb with misery, she stood and let the words of Dora's rage hit her like arrows.

'Stupid, hysterical kids—'

A cat jumped up on the table and started on the egg as Dora grabbed her jacket from the hook behind the door and slammed out.

Callie followed.

'What do you want?' Dora flung angrily over her shoulder as she ran.

'Can't I help you look for them?'

'I suppose so. I've no idea where to start. Have to follow the hoof tracks. Is there anything left we can ride?'

'All gone except Dottie and Polly.'

'Oh God.' The vision of Callie and Dora setting off to the rescue on the little brown donkey and her foal might have made her laugh, but it didn't. She strode ahead. Callie trotted after. There was nothing else to do.

They ran down the slope, crossed the stream at the bottom and began to push through the bushes that thickened the end of the field. As they came out to where they could see the gate, Dora stopped and let out a yell of laughter. Callie stopped and stared. Then all the anguish and the fear and the guilt from Dora's anger suddenly exploded into the relief of a wild, high-pitched crowing laughter. For a moment, they could only stand there, clutching each other, cackling with joy.

Outside the gate, lined up like people at a cafeteria, were all the old horses, Cobbler's Dream in the lead, the others behind him in order of rank, Robin modestly near the end as a new-comer, waiting patiently for someone to come and let them in for breakfast.

Walking back up the field with the horses, Callie said, 'What about Steve? He'll hear the horses coming in.'

'I could say that I went out late last night and turned them out after we knew there was no danger.'

In the kitchen, an hour ago, it had seemed as if Callie and Dora could never be friends again. But really nothing had changed. Dora was still the kind of friend who could under-stand when you wanted something hushed up.

'But he'd have heard them going out, if so,' Callie said. 'That's why I led them out quietly, one by one.'

'All right. I led them out quietly one by one.'

When Dora went into the kitchen after finishing the morn-ing's work with Callie and Steve, her egg plate was still on the table, polished so clean by rough cat tongues that it appeared never to have been used.

' 'Lo, Dora.' The Colonel, who should have been looking joyful, was looking gloomy. He had his old clacketty type-writer on the table, and was banging on it with one finger of each hand, his unlit pipe in the corner of his mouth, his giant size coffee cup that Anna had brought back from Italy beside him, just such a cosy domestic scene as Dora had imagined when she was homesick in Mrs Blank's spick and span kitchen.

'I'm writing to Blankenheimer,' he said. 'I've held off until I saw what was what, but now I have to write and tell him what I think of him.'

'But why?' Dora sat down and spread her hands beseechingly on the table. 'Why? Now that it doesn't matter any more?'

'Not matter?' The Colonel looked at her over the half glasses he wore for reading. 'But it's a question of principle, don't you see? There's a law been broken. There's a fishy deal been done. It's the act, not the consequences that matters. Don't you see?' he asked again.

Dora sighed and did not answer. Most of the time at Folly-foot it seemed as if age did not matter, as if everyone – Slugger, Anna and the Colonel, Steve and Dora, Callie – were the same generation, with a common purpose and a common pleasure centred on horses. But when something like this came up – forget it. If she said what she thought, the Colonel would say she was immoral.

'False papers,' the Colonel said, shaking his head glumly. 'I don't know what the immigration authorities will make of this, but it could land our friend Blankenheimer in very serious trouble.'

He had his hands raised to strike the keys again, like an arthritic pianist, but Dora got up and shouted. There was no other way to do it. It was the thought of darling Blank, innocent and kind, the most generous gift of his life shattered, just as if Robin were a precious porcelain horse shattered by careless packers. It was the vision of Blank getting out of his comfortable car at the post office, finding the letter in his mail box – 'Hey, great! A letter from the Colonel. Look, Mary, a letter from my old British buddy' – and then his face under whatever funny cap he was wearing now, stricken with the realization of what Chuckie and Dora had done to him. That was why she had to shout.

'It wasn't him!' she shouted. 'It was Chuckie Fiske and me. We were the only ones who knew. Yes, of course I knew.' She wouldn't let him speak, because if she stopped, she might not get started again. 'I didn't tell you because I was afraid you'd be angry. Well, you are angry and I am afraid. But Blank knew nothing, and I'm not going to let you accuse him, do you hear?'

'What's all the shouting?' Anna came in and Dora went out, on fire. She could almost see her nostrils steaming.

She had done what she had to do. She had stopped the Colonel writing to Blank, but now all his anger would be directed at her. She didn't know that she could bear the weight of it.

She tried to keep out of his way. When she did not come in for supper on the second day, Steve went to look for her. He found her in Robin's stable, her arm round his neck and her face in his fine black mane. Robin was paying more attention to his food than to her, in the comforting way horses have of showing you that the world hasn't come to an end.

'Aren't you coming in for supper?' Steve put his hand on her arm, lightly, because Dora didn't always want to be touched when she was upset.

'I can't eat.'

'Well, that's a lie,' Steve said candidly, 'since I saw you sitting on the wall this morning with a chunk of bread and butter in each fist.'

'I can't be in a room with the Colonel, if he still hates me.'

'Who says he hates you? Don't you know the difference between hate and anger? He'll get over it.'

'Never.'

'All right, love.' Steve went to the door. 'Don't believe me. Just wait and see.'

twenty-eight

The chalky hills rolled away on either side of Follyfoot Farm, following the lines of some ancient upheaval in the foundations of Britain. There were villages in the folds between the hills, some grazing farms and a few isolated houses in bare and windy spots, rugged, thick-walled, headed into the view.

About ten miles from Follyfoot, there was a small cottage, once painted white, now rusty where the paint had flaked and the old bricks showed through. What had once been a good vegetable garden was now sadly neglected. Only a few cabbages and lettuces gone to seed grew among the weeds and broken pea sticks.

But behind the house in the sheltering beechwood, the source of a stream bubbled up through tender bright green water plants. In front stretched the breathtaking view of gently diminishing hills, fields of all colour, farms, churches, curving roads, the willowed line of the river far away.

Mabel had fallen in love with the place as soon as she saw it. Her children hated it. That confirmed Mabel's opinion.

Mabel's husband had died a long time ago when her children were small. When her father died, her old mother moved in with her. She became more and more difficult as she grew older. The children objected to taking care of her when Mabel was out. She fell in the fire and wandered off down the road at night.

The day she almost got run over by the late bus, everybody told Mabel that her mother must go into a nursing home. The old lady was last seen being wheeled away down a corridor, calling back feebly, 'Don't leave me, Mabel!'

Mabel's children got married and had children of their own, and grew more opinionated and efficient and busy. Sometimes they seemed like strangers, who could never have been the dreamy children she had hugged. Mabel herself gradually became an old lady. She began to forget things, to stumble and lose her glasses, and repeat herself, and set fire to pans of bacon fat on the stove.

She realized that her children, particularly the girls, had begun to look at each other and mutter, and she thought that they were plotting to do the same thing to her as she had done to her mother.

But she could never go to a home, because she had dogs and cats, not to mention her old horse, who had been with her longer than anyone could remember. She had a bit of money saved, and she knew what she would do.

She sat her children down and said to them, 'I'm getting near the end of my life.'

'Oh nonsense, Mother,' Rachel said automatically. 'You've got years yet.'

'I'm going to do what I've always wanted.' Mabel ignored her. 'I'm going to take my animals and find a small cottage miles away from anywhere, and you don't have to keep coming to see me, because I don't want you to.'

'But we must. We'd feel—'

'Don't come for your sakes,' Mabel said. 'If you come at all, come for mine. If I want you, I'll send for you.'

'Will you ring us up every day? Once a week?'

'No. Because I shan't have a telephone.'

'Then how can you send for us? Letters take ages. If you were ill—'

'I'll manage. You'll know,' Mabel said mysteriously. She had become more mysterious and weird in her old age.

*

Against her children's protest, Mabel bought the small cottage facing the marvellous view. Between the back garden and the beechwood was a good small paddock with an open shed for her old horse. This horse's name was Julian, after her lover, who had been killed in the First World War. Her children considered it pretty bad taste of her not to have called him Sidney after her husband.

Julian was about twenty-two years old. He was a bit of an old crock, but could still pull the dog cart to the village when Mabel needed food. He was not a lovable horse. He had a small moustache on his top lip and hips like a cow, and a cautious way of setting his ears straight up with the insides turned sideways and showing the yellow of his eye. But he and Mabel understood each other, and his legs had served her faithfully long after her own had left her in the lurch.

One wet afternoon, Dora took Robin out for a long ride. It was the one thing that helped. Riding him was still the same pure, exhilarating pleasure that it had been in America, but more so now, because he was hers, and she could teach him things that would be for the two of them alone.

She rode along the old grassed-over Roman road just below the top of the hills, in and out of the small valleys, jumping streams, cantering tirelessly on the short turf that squelched up little fountains under Robin's hoofs. Each time she thought of turning back, she wanted to go farther. It would be a long way home, but she didn't care.

Something let go. She lurched to one side as the stirrup leather split through at the fold. Cleaning tack was not one of the strong points of Follyfoot. The dried out leather had been cracking through for a long time.

A bit of string and a sharp skewer would do it. When Dora passed a gate half off its hinges, she turned down the lane between beech trees and found a cottage with an old horse who gave Robin an unenthusiastic greeting, and an old lady in a dark rain cape with a hood messing about in a neglected vegetable plot.

'Could I possibly borrow some string?' Dora rode near to her.

The old lady looked at Robin with pleasure, and at the stirrup leather with tut-tuts. 'Your stuff is in almost as bad shape as mine.' When she smiled, she didn't look so much like a witch.

She brought out some string and a sharp skewer to poke holes in the two ends of the leather, then took her to admire the old horse before Dora left. It was raining quite hard. The horse was standing in the middle of the field with his ears back and his tail tucked in. The old lady chased him into the shed and put up the bars.

'Do you have far to go home?' she asked Dora.

'About ten miles. I needed a long ride. Bad things have been happening. I just had to get off on my own.'

'I know what you mean,' said the old lady. 'There were bad things for me too. Julian and I had to get away by ourselves.'

'I like it here,' Dora said.

'Come back.' The old lady was shivering. She started towards the house. 'My name is Mabel. I'll give you some cocoa and some of the awful bread I bake. I'm not quite up to it today.'

After the girl with the beautiful horse had gone, Mabel went into the house and lit the fire and fed the dogs and cats and sat in the chair which fitted her shape like a comforting hand. One of the cats jumped on her lap. She folded her hands across its broad grey back, and enjoyed some memories.

Perhaps, she thought, I will send a message to the girls. I really don't feel up to much today. If I am going to be ill, it would be only fair to let them know. They'd feel guilty. Shut up, Mabel, she told herself. It was to get away from useless things like guilt that you came up here.

Dora thought quite a bit about Mabel and her lonely cottage, and about being old and wanting to be left alone. Mabel didn't have to worry what people thought of her because there were no people.

Dora was still padding round, trying to keep out of the Colonel's way or trying to please him and doing everything wrong. Spilling his coffee, losing a bill for oats, leaving a rake upturned in a dark corner, where Sir Richard Wortley trod on the prongs and got konked in the forehead by the handle.

Steve found her saddling Robin.

'Where are you going?'

'Oh – for a ride.'

'When will you be back? I'm not going to start mending that roof unless you're going to help me.'

'I'm going a long way.'

'Then I'll come. Miss needs the work. We'll do the roof when we get back.'

'But—' But why not? Mabel hadn't minded Dora coming to the house. It was mostly her daughters she didn't want.

It was a glorious ride. The sun was in and out. A week of rain had drawn out all the spicy fragrance of the bushes and low clumpy plants that grew along the hills. When the horses got into the rhythm of a long canter together, it felt as if it could go on for ever.

'Remember the last ride you had with me?' Steve said as they pulled up to cross a chalky rock slide.

Dora rubbed her head. 'Almost was my last ride with any-one. Poor Rebel. I wonder what the Crowleys think about it all?'

'Just as long as they don't think about getting another bargain horse.'

'They will.'

'And you'll end up with it at Follyfoot.'

'Probably. I don't know though.' Dora thought of the Colonel. 'Have to be someone else's idea next time.'

As they rode down the lane under the roofing beeches, they heard a pandemonium of barking from the little house. Dora called Mabel, and when there was no answer, she gave Robin's reins to Steve and tried the back door. As she opened it, the dogs surged out and ran off, barking in a crazy way.

The kitchen was chaotic. Food pulled out of the cupboards, milk bottles tipped over, cat and dog mess everywhere.

Dora went out again. 'Steve. Tie the horses up and come in.'

They went through to the front room. In the doorway, Steve instinctively put his arm out and said, 'Don't look.'

'I'm not afraid.'

Mabel was sitting in a chair by the empty fireplace. She seemed to have been dead for several days.

Shut in the shed by the bars, Julian had been pawing futilely at the ground underneath them, but was now propped in a far corner, barely able to stand. He had obviously had no food or water for some time. He was terribly dehydrated.

They gave him a small amount of food and water to start with, locked the back door of the house and took the key, and went to telephone a doctor, and for the horse box to come for Julian.

In the lane, they met a car, full of women and children. There was only one house at the end of this road. It must be Mabel's family.

They stood their horses in the middle of the lane. The driver leaned out to tell them to move aside. Dora rode closer.

'Are you going to see Mabel?'

'Yes. Who are you? We're her family. Thought we'd stop by and see how she is.'

Dora could only stare, so Steve said, 'It's too late.'

'What do you mean?'

'She's dead.'

'Oh, my God!' The two women made fluttery movements of trying to put hands over children's ears. The children jerked away and listened solemnly.

'My God, how ghastly!'

'No,' Dora said. 'It's all right. She wanted to die like that, I think. No fuss. Off on her own.'

The hard-faced daughter with the glistening scarlet mouth said in a shocked sort of tone, 'Last week, I was woken up by a voice quite close. It said "Rachel". I didn't pay any attention. I thought it was my conscience. She always said, "I'll send for you if I need you." I thought she meant telephone or letter. I didn't know she meant like that.'

Dora gave them the key and left them to ring the doctor, the police, the ambulance – they were arguing who it should be as Dora and Steve rode on. In the village, Dora telephoned the Colonel to send the horse box.

'Another customer, Dora?' He sounded like his old self.

'Yes. He's quite old and he's weak. He's been starved for days, but I think we can save him.'

'Good girl,' the Colonel said. 'Well done. You do seem to find just the horses that Follyfoot is here for.'

Everything was all right. Although she was still shaky from the shock of Mabel, Dora came out of the telephone box feeling as if a dark cloud had lifted. Wait – there was one nagging unease. What was it? Oh yes. She had thought she was the only person who heard voices in the night. Bit disappointing to find that a girdled woman with stiff hair and lipstick like blood heard them too.

twenty-nine

Every year as autumn approached, Callie organized a celebration for all the neighbourhood animals that had been born that summer.

Puppies, kittens, chickens, ducks, geese, fish in bowls, an abandoned fledgling Toby had found, who had refused to leave as it grew feathers and strength, and spent a lot of time in Toby's pocket.

Dottie and her foal Polka Dot, a prize exhibit. Folly, because it wasn't fair to exclude him for being born two months before spring. Three leggy young Dartmoors from the pony farm. Moll's calico cat's fifty-ninth kitten. Toby's mother's new baby. A box of young Belgian rabbits. A pair of hound pups who were being 'walked' by Mrs Oldcastle.

Everybody got a prize, because no one was better than anyone else.

Robin was allowed to enter because he had been reborn as a British citizen. Julian was celebrated because he had been born again – snatched from the jaws of death.

There was always something to celebrate at Follyfoot.

What they were really celebrating was life.

Monica Dickens
Follyfoot 40p

Here we meet for the first time the people and horses who live at the
farm on the top of the hill. There's always so much to do on the farm —
tending unwanted horses, providing mounts for film companies,
schooling ponies, helping unlucky holidaymakers — and keeping a wary
eye on the unscrupulous owners of the Pinecrest riding stables!

Dora at Follyfoot 40p

More exciting adventures at the Follyfoot farm! This time, the Captain
has to go away and he leaves everything in the charge of Dora and
Steve, warning them — with an eye on the finances — 'Don't buy any
more horses!' But Dora knows she just has to buy Amigo, the rangy,
scarred, cream-coloured horse, even if it means borrowing money . . .

The House at World's End 35p

Rather than stay with relations in a grey London suburb, the Fielding
children, Tom, Carrie, Em and Michael, decide to live by themselves in
a tumbledown country pub. There are thrilling moments and frightening
ones, too, as the house at World's End becomes a haven for sick, stray
or ill-treated animals.

Spring Comes to World's End 35p

As their Uncle Rudolph threatens to deprive them of their beloved
World's End, the Fielding children try to earn the money to buy it
themselves. But money disappears as fast as it comes in, and it is not
until the children are at the point of despair that their home is saved in
a dramatic and exciting climax.

Summer at World's End 35p

The Fielding children are still on their own, still caring for any animal
in distress. Lack of money is a problem while some unwanted visitors
add to the fun — and the excitement.

Eric Delderfield
True Animal Stories 35p

Fascinating stories about animals of all kinds – cows, deer, squirrels, badgers, elephants and monkeys – as well as the more usual domestic pets. From the tortoise who travelled by air to the goose who went to sea, all these stories are as true and as varied as the animals themselves.

Second Book of True Animal Stories 35p

Another fascinating book of stories about animals of all kinds; the stories are as varied as the animals themselves, dolphins, tigers, donkeys, foxes and others. Also read about safari parks and lion reserves. Some of the best stories are about: the deep friendship between a hen and a cat, the Jack Russell terrier who always answers the phone, the lion who takes his master for a walk and the hospital where 38,000 animals are treated every year.

Jacquelyn Berrill
The World of Wolves 30p

This book tells the true life history of the wolf, and explains away some of the myths about it being such a ferocious animal. The author has written an informative account of this fascinating creature, and she also drew the beautiful illustrations.

You can buy these and other Piccolo books from booksellers and newsagents; or direct from the following address:
Pan Books, Sales Office, Cavaye Place, London SW10 9PG
Send purchase price plus 20p for the first book and 10p for each additional book, to allow for postage and packing
Prices quoted are applicable in UK

While every effort is made to keep prices low, it is sometimes necessary to increase prices at short notice. Pan Books reserve the right to show on covers new retail prices which may differ from those advertised in the text or elsewhere.